The Magic Singer

a visionary fantasy

by
JoAnn J. Elliot

The Magic Singer

ISBN: 978-1-7343838-0-5

Sing A World Media
Publisher

Layout & graphic assistance by WBC Design

Printed in the United States of America
by Kindle Direct Publishing,
an Amazon company

PROLOGUE

Once upon a time, in the world of Melodus, the Secret Valley was not a secret. Men, women and children lived happily there in the midst of the Melody Mountains with the fairies and gnomes as their helpers. The Magic Singer wove coats of music that enfolded them and their valley.

Over the centuries, many people became curious about the rest of the land. They moved from the Secret Valley to the valley of Spring Gate outside the Melody Mountains. After a while some ventured further beyond into the wider world of Melodus.

When the people first came out of the mountains they were shining and fair to behold. Their reflections in lakes and quiet streams certainly told them so. Mirrors were invented so people could admire themselves all day long.

Slowly, so slowly that few realized it, they forgot the Singer and the song. They forgot their little helpers. One day they looked in the mirror and saw but an ordinary person.

Something was missing, but what?

Rules were made to give certainty to life. Each rule was threaded with the same theme: life was ordinary, so nothing too exciting should happen and people were ordinary, so no one should shine brighter than another. The Secret Valley, the Magic Singer, the little folk, became the Melody Tales, studied by eccentric scholars and sung about by the traveling singers, but scorned by most folks as nonsense.

In recent years reports came from the lands beyond Spring Gate that creeks were drying up and crops failing. Some people actually ate less than three good meals a day. But that took place somewhere else. Surely nothing would happen in Spring Gate.

Something had to happen, though, for better or worse.

One day the songwind fairies hovered over Tunetall Peak in the Melody Mountains. Music hummed within their dresses. Wisps of pink and green garments curled around tiny bodies and blended with the crest of the mountain wind.

The wind carried the fairies down the snowy peak and past the rivulets that merged into Sweetwater Creek at the foot of the mountain. It rushed between the pine treed hills to the outer, smoother hills that circled Spring Gate and then lost its frosty nip. Now the fairies tidied their dresses and left the arms of the wind. They flew into the tamer valley with its strictly-pruned trees and regimented fields.

When the fairies reached the village of Spring Gate, they searched the shops, the school and the homes. They found her.

She had started watering the tulips and narcissus in the flower box outside her bedroom window but she had stopped and was gazing sadly at the mountains. The fairies drifted up to the window and then danced, letting their dresses swish against her. The girl couldn't see or feel the fairies but she laughed, put down her watering can and leaning her elbows on the windowsill, she began to dream. Her dreams shone, like the Secret Valley within the Melody Mountains. Yes, they had found her.

Chapter
One

SUSANNA DREAMS
WHILE AUNT PRUDENCE PROPOSES

Fidelity, the fairy, gathered her blue dress around her, spun into the air and flew to the Mansfield house. This had been her daily assignment for the past year. Fidelity reviewed the picture in her mind. If the picture changed she would have to report at once to her chief in the Secret Valley.

Watching and listening, she circled the house. The voices of Aunt Prudence and Aunt Maisy drifted out of the parlor window.

"Did her father give me complete guardianship over her or not?" demanded Aunt Prudence.

"Yes...but," stammered Aunt Maisy.

"Don't you think I know what's right for her?"

"Well...sometimes, yes, but..."

"Enough of your buts. She must be toned down. It's for her own good. Burl is the only man who would possibly marry her. Erna Ringwurst trained him to be the perfect example of an ordinary young man. He does nothing to stir up excitement and when he does speak, he uses excellent flat tones."

"But I don't want her toned down. I like her the way she is," said Aunt Maisy.

"I'm fond of her too, but unless she blends in she'll become an outcast. We owe it to her to get her betrothed to Burl right away. Her coming-of-age birthday is in less than two months. We'll have to work swiftly."

"Perhaps Erna won't want her in her family," said Aunt Maisy.

"You realize Erna is our only chance to get Susanna married and looked after? The other families with sons wouldn't consider her. She's too unusual. I'm sure Erna will jump at the chance to show people her dear son is capable of toning Susanna down. You know the old saying: 'only the pinnacle of ordinary can tone down the most unusual'. Erna wants to be the pinnacle of ordinary. Also, I'll hint that Susanna is an excellent housekeeper just like us. Our housekeeping has been what's saved us from being outcasts, what with the males in our family always reading those Melody Tales and making themselves ridiculous by talking about them. Good housekeeping with no frills is the best of ordinary. Now, I shall get together with Erna and propose this. "

"Oh Prudence, let Susanna stay with us for a while longer. You know how fragile she is, she might not do well under Erna's thumb."

"Absolutely not! My mind is made up. She'll have to obey me or else. I won't take the chance of her being left by herself when we die. It's possible she might live longer than we expect."

The beautiful picture in Fidelity's mind wobbled and its colors grew dull. This was exactly how a threat could affect the image. She spun herself into a tight spiral and whizzed through the air back to the Secret Valley.

Three days later, Aunt Maisy closed the workshop door behind her. She leaned back and looked towards the house with a small, determined smile on her face.

"Aunt Maisy," said a voice beside her.

She jumped and put her hand on her heart. "Susanna, don't sneak up on me like that."

"I've been looking all over for you. What were you doing in Father's old workshop?"

"I've leased it to a carpenter for one year."

"You have! What will Aunt Prudence say?"

"It doesn't matter what she says. She may be in charge of

you but we own this property equally. Besides, the carpenter paid a handsome fee." Aunt Maisy jingled the coins in her apron pocket. "That should keep her quiet."

"Aunt Maisy," said Susanna, "I have to tell you about the dream I had last night. It's the best yet."

Susanna took her aunt's arm and led her through the apple orchard to the broken pillar and crumbling stones beside the fir tree. Aunt Maisy sat carefully on the pillar but Susanna stood, her blue eyes sparkling with excitement.

"Aunt Maisy, oh Aunt Maisy, I saw a beautiful woman in my dream last night *and* she's the one who's been singing those songs I heard in the other dreams."

"That's nice dear."

"Nice? It's extraordinary! This dream was alive and…I believe the woman is real, so I'm going to find her."

"Are you sure dear? Don't be hasty. Dreams are just… well, they're just dreams."

"The Melody Tales talk about people going on quests to find magic. That's what I'm going to do—go on a quest."

"Susanna dear, surely it can't be that important?"

"Oh yes it is! Remember I told you how I was watering my flowers a year ago and one moment I felt unhappy and the next moment I felt glad to be alive? What I didn't tell you was, that moment was as stupendous as the day Aunt Prudence gave me Father's Melody Tales. I know she had to do it because she'd promised him she would as soon as I was ten. Thank goodness she believes in keeping her word. Well, this time last year I'd been about to give in and forget about my beautiful world. I could feel two worlds calling out to me."

"Two worlds? My dear, what are you talking about? Did you hurt your head, were you seeing double?"

"No, you don't understand. The beautiful one seemed inside me and gave me wonderful feelings. The other one was this outside ordinary world where nothing makes sense even though there are lots of rules. It was hard to believe in my inner world when no one else did. I was beginning to think I'd imagined it, so I was planning to forget it and be like Gerda Thompson, the paragon of ordinary virtues. I figured I'd probably die young anyway, just like mother and father, so why not give in and be like everyone else. But all of a sudden I felt happy and certain my inner world was real. After that day I began to hear the beautiful melodies in my dreams. I must find that singer because she's the most amazing person I've ever seen. Her songs tickle a wonderful spot in my heart."

She sat down on the stone next to Aunt Maisy and leaned closer. "And do you know what else? I think she's the Magic Singer the Melody Tales talk about. She's supposed to have a gown made from ribbons of song and her melodies make the creeks run full all summer long."

"Susanna, you make my head spin. I'm sure there's only one world, dear. You know the Melody Tales are nonsense. You have too much imagination and that's what makes you restless and dissatisfied. I've found enough in this world to keep me busy. You know I love to cook. I can get quite excited over a new recipe. Your father loved my cooking. Of course, when he married, your mother helped me, and I will confess, she had a way of getting flavor into dishes that I never figured out. Just stay home and find something to keep you busy. That's my advice. Oh no, here comes Prudence."

"Maisy!" shouted Aunt Prudence, storming through the apple orchard and then planting herself in front of her. "There's a strange young man in the workshop and he won't leave. He told me he gave you some gold. Now, what's this about?"

Aunt Maisy stood up and lifted her chin defiantly, although it did tremble. She reached into her apron pocket and took out all the coins. She counted out half and put those back.

"Since we divide our profits," she said, putting out her hand with the gleaming gold towards Aunt Prudence, "here's your share."

"Aunt Prudence," said Susanna, standing up. "Now you

can afford some new yarn. Remember you wanted a blue color for a shawl."

"She can make several shawls and a lot more with this," said Aunt Maisy. "The carpenter is a fine gentleman. When he described the furniture he makes, I could smell the fresh wood shavings and hear a hammer and saw at work. It would be just like when Susanna's father was alive."

"Well," said Aunt Prudence, staring at the gold, "you should have discussed it with me first. I'm quite upset about that and…did you include meals?"

"He said he'd cook for himself and live in the workshop so we wouldn't have to put him up."

"All right," said Aunt Prudence, taking the coins and dropping them into her apron pocket. "He can stay. But if there's any trouble, I'll send him packing. Susanna, you go in and get your shawl. The air still has a chill in it. Go on, we can't have you catching a cold. You know you probably have the weak lungs of your mother and father. I won't have you dying of pneumonia too."

"I'll get it in a moment. When you're ready to choose your yarn, let me help you. I've a good eye for color."

"If I let you choose I'd end up with a blue so bright I'd be embarrassed to wear it in public."

"I'll show you the blue I'm thinking of. One of Mother's old ribbons has the perfect shade. She must have had a dress that color."

"Susanna, I appreciate your help, I do, but you have no idea which colors are appropriate. Now go in and get your shawl."

"Oh yes I do. You take any color and muddy it with enough brown to make it dull. But you'd really suit the blue I'm thinking of…oh, very well, I'll get my shawl."

The aunts watched her stride through the apple orchard, tripping over a tree root, as usual.

"And you want to marry her off to Burl Ringwurst," said Aunt Maisy.

"You stay out of this Maisy. That gold is making you awfully pushy. Don't you dare tell Susanna. I need to handle her just right. She can be so stubborn."

"I think her stubbornness is good. If she'd given in to you when her father and mother died she'd be called Sue and she is not a Sue. You couldn't even get her to compromise with Susan."

"That's exactly what I'm talking about. Imagine her telling me I could starve her to death and she'd still not answer. As if I'd have done that! I gave in then but I won't give in with this marriage. It's much more important than a fancy name."

Chapter
Two

NEWCOMERS BEARING GIFTS

"Susanna, answer the front door, please," said Aunt Prudence, "I need to keep stirring the porridge or it'll go lumpy. Maisy took the carpenter his breakfast. She said it's a onetime treat but I don't believe that for a moment. She's dying to have a man to spoil, like she did your father."

When she opened the door, Fidelity whisked her slender six inches up to her and kissed her cheek—unseen and unfelt. The morning sun shone in Susanna's eyes and all she saw was a tall silhouette standing on the porch.

"Good morning," said the silhouette. "Sorry to bother you so early but I couldn't wait to see you again. I only just moved in. My goodness…you look just like your mother when she was your age. I'm your Aunt Violet."

"You are!" said Susanna, squinting to see her. "Oh, how splendid! I've always wanted to meet you. Your letters on my birthdays have meant a lot to me. Sometimes you would say something that sounded like it was right out of the Melody Tales. Come on in." She directed her aunt into the parlor, for she was trained by Aunt Prudence to leave only male callers on the doorstep. After seating her on the sofa Susanna sat down on the straight-backed chair beside the window. Fidelity perched on the windowsill and gazed at Susanna with adoring eyes.

The silhouette had filled in with a green dress—a quiet but not a dull green. A thick braid of red hair fell down her back to her waist.

"Do you still make your jellies?" asked Susanna.

"Oh, yes," said Aunt Violet. "It's a treat to see you, my dear. You look so like my sister, the same blue eyes and the same luscious hair. Glorianna always had trouble getting her hair to stay behind her ears when she wore it down. The mouth is the same too, very generous—a good mouth for singing."

"Violet...it is you!" exclaimed Aunt Prudence coming into the room. "I thought your voice sounded familiar. You haven't been here since Susanna's birth. Whatever are you doing here now?"

"I just moved into Spring Gate," said Violet. "Last night, in fact, in that lovely house down by the fork in the creek."

"You moved into my best friend Amy's house," said Susanna. "That's the most wonderful place. It looks right through the gap in the hills. In her last letter she said they'd rented it to someone but she didn't know who. They're coming back in about a year, you know. They had to help their relatives in Harlowville as their general store isn't doing well because of the drought on the plains. It's cheaper to have family working in the store—you don't have to pay them."

"That's enough of someone else's private affairs, Susanna," said Aunt Prudence. "Now, excuse me for asking, but why have you decided to move here after all these years?"

"I decided I wanted to be with Susanna, even if only for a few months. I would have come sooner, to watch you grow up, my dear, but my business wouldn't let me. I have a thriving jelly business: "Violet's Noteworthy Jellies". And I brought you something which I hope you like."

Violet stood up and pulled a long shawl out of her bag. The color was an unobtrusive yellow with flecks of blue. She swirled it over Aunt Prudence's shoulders. Fidelity hovered above the bag watching Violet.

"There," said Violet, "I knew it would look perfect on you—just a touch of blue to match your eyes. The yellow is such a suitable bland color, isn't it? I knitted another one with pink highlights for Maisy."

After Violet drew out Aunt Maisy's shawl, Fidelity dove into the bag and tugged on a ball of yarn of the finest thread of pink light. She grabbed the end of the yarn in one tiny hand and flew round and round Susanna from shoulders to ankles. Her flying was so swift that it looked like a gossamer garment was being painted over Susanna. When the ball of yarn was unwound, Susanna wore a floor length cloak and Fidelity was walking around her adjusting the hem and singing a song:

Wearing this cloak you now shall hear
The song of your dreams ever near,
Wafting gently into your mind
During the day, at any time.
It shall lead you on and on
By the beauty of its song,
Till' you find that perfect place
Where fear cannot leave a trace.

No one noticed what was going on except Violet who gave Fidelity a wink. The pink cloak shimmered for a moment and then dissolved into Susanna's body. She and Fidelity both gave a deep sigh.

Aunt Prudence looked startled with her gift but after a few blinks she rubbed an end of the shawl against her cheek. "Yes, it's very nice. Thank you, that's so thoughtful. What an interesting pattern. I'm sure I've never seen it before."

Violet reached into her bag again and brought out two small jars. "More gifts—jelly, of course. This is 'Raspberry Rhapsody' and 'Peppy Pear'. I hope you enjoy them with your breakfast."

"Yes, breakfast, of course," said Aunt Prudence. "You must join us. Susanna, lead the way into the kitchen. I'll be with you as soon as I've put our new shawls in a safe place."

Later, after Aunt Violet had left, Susanna wiped out the dishpan and then poured hot water from the kettle over the dishcloth. Fidelity sat happily on her shoulder while she hung the cloth on its brass hook. Susanna paused as the melody from her dreams wafted into her mind like the unwinding of a ribbon of sunlight.

"I can't tell what that extra something is that makes this jelly so delicious," said Aunt Maisy, sitting at the table and tasting Violet's raspberry jelly with a tiny spoon. "What did she give you, dear?"

"Oh…nothing," said Susanna, sighing because the melody faded. "I never realized it until you mentioned it."

"That's odd," said Aunt Prudence, pressing the tea towels on the ironing board beside the stove. "I mean, you above all of us should have been given a present. Nothing against your mother and her family, dear, but she was a traveling singer and nice as their singing is, there's always something different about them. You can't expect them to behave like us."

"I feel like I got a present," said Susanna, while Fidelity helped her tug a length of hair behind her ear. "I don't know why, I just do."

"And I don't know why I agreed to let you help her in the afternoons to get settled. Maisy and I will certainly be shorthanded. Well, no matter how odd she is, she's still family and I shall do my duty. However, young lady, you're to help me every morning to get ready for the tea I've planned for the Ringwursts. They just acknowledged my invitation for a week from tomorrow. I want you to be nice to Burl, just be yourself, but make sure you pay attention to him."

"That's like asking me to pay attention to the sofa."

"What a rude thing to say about that fine young man."

"I only mean he's so bland that he blends right in with the furniture. I'm sure he has all the necessary virtues, but really, Aunt Prudence, whenever I think of him, which is only about every second year, I start to yawn."

"Susanna, I won't allow you to talk about him like that. It's time you recognized that blending is the most important thing in life. However, I'm not asking you to act differently, just talk to him."

"All right, I'll try to engage him in conversation. It'll be hard to enlarge on 'yes', 'no' and 'you don't say', but I'll do my best."

Chapter
Three

GIDEON DOESN'T WANT TO BE A FRIEND

Susanna closed the back door behind her and listened. Good, she thought, the aunts are in the parlor. Now she could introduce herself to the new carpenter.

She walked along the short path through the trees that led to the workshop. Fidelity had already flown ahead of her and waited by the door. The carpenter was singing. He had an everyday sort of voice but it sounded effortless and easy on her ears. She waited for a moment and then knocked.

The door opened. Gustafus, the gnome, stood there and then shook his head in disgust. These people never noticed him. He could understand them not noticing fairies. After all, Fidelity was only six inches, but he topped three feet—without his shoes. Why he had ever volunteered to come to such a backward place, he didn't know. He stomped over to the wheel that turned the lathe.

Susanna peered into the dimmer light of the workshop and saw the carpenter outlined against the far window. The door must not have been latched properly, she thought. He had stopped singing and was looking in her direction. Gosh, he was not much older than she. When he walked up to her and looked down into her eyes, she heard him catch his breath.

"How do you do," she said, extending her hand. "I thought I should come and introduce myself. I'm Susanna. This was my father's workshop. What's your name?"

"Gideon," he said, taking her hand in his and holding it, no shaking, just a firm, warm holding. Fidelity squeezed her hands together in delight as she hovered between them.

"More than two syllables," said Susanna, "I love names

with lots of syllables. If you have more than two around here people think you're getting above yourself. My mother had four syllables in her name. You should let go of my hand now. Aunt Prudence says a handshake with a man must be brief. You have an awfully nice singing voice. You aren't a traveling singer are you?"

He released her hand and smiled. "No, I just like to sing as I work."

"My mother was a traveling singer and her voice was beautiful. Yours is like hers, I mean, because it comes out so easily. Where did you come from?"

Gustafus started to turn the lathe's wheel but Gideon shook his head slightly so he let go of the wheel's handle. He then tromped over to the chair by the pot bellied stove and sat down, his arms folded in disapproval. Fidelity flew to him and sat on the arm of the chair.

Gideon walked to the lathe and brushed off some shavings on the furniture leg held in the vise. "I'm from Songward. You know where that is, don't you?"

"Of course, my mother was from there. That's where the traveling singers come from. I'd like to see it someday. I remember she said it was straight west of here but way on the other side of the mountains. No one goes through the mountains, so it must have taken you a long time to get here. You could use someone to help you turn the wheel, couldn't you? I used to turn it for my father. What do you make?"

"I make cupboards, small ones with ornate legs and fancy trimmings. I find the most unusual wood I can and then let it tell me what style of cupboard it wants to be. Look at this piece. What do you think it wants to be?"

He moved over to the long bench under the window and picked up a slab of wood. Susanna watched him in wonder. She had never seen such a handsome man before and he didn't even try to be handsome. His chestnut brown hair was swept behind his ears—and stayed there, she noted. His hair and eyes made her think of summer sunshine—sunshine burnishing a rich earth and sunshine lighting up a friendly sky. Fidelity nodded a meaningful glance at Gustafus.

"Well, what do you think?" asked Gideon.

"Of what? Oh yes, what kind of cupboard. This is unusual wood. It's…purple! The grain looks like a bluish purple—how beautiful." She moved her hand slowly over the wood's rich surface. "It wants to be…a small shelf for a complete set of the Melody Tales. I know it does—just the size to go on the top of a bureau. Trouble is I'm the only one I know who has a set. Mine are in the top drawer of my bureau. Aunt Prudence lets out a huge sigh whenever she sees one, so I keep them out of sight as much as I can. I do have a favor to ask of you though, if you don't mind, and you'll have to keep it a secret from my aunts. You won't need to use any fancy wood for it. It just has to be sturdy. I can pay you."

"I'm at your service. What do you need?"

"I need a wheelbarrow," she said, looking down and drawing a pattern on the wooden floor with the toe of her shoe.

"Didn't I see one in the barn?"

"Yes."

"Isn't there another one beneath an apple tree?"

"Probably."

Gideon watched her with one raised eyebrow.

She lifted her head and looked at him defiantly. "I want my own."

"Why?"

"It's a secret."

"I always have to know why I'm making a piece of furniture or in this case, a sturdy wheelbarrow."

Susanna marched to the door of the workshop and put her hand on the latch.

"I would keep your secret, Susanna."

She walked back and looked up at him with her hands clasped in front of her heart. "I'm going on a quest. It's the most important thing I've ever done in my whole life. The wheelbarrow will carry the supplies I need. I won't borrow the ones we have—they need them here. I can't take our only horse and I know I'd get awfully tired carrying things on my back. So, I figured a wheelbarrow would be just the thing."

"A quest for what?"

"For the most beautiful, the most amazing woman I've ever seen. She must be the Magic Singer, the one in the Melody Tales. I hear her music in my dreams and I can never remember it when I get up, except for today—the melody just flew into my mind as I was finishing the dishes. It actually tastes delicious—well, taste is the closest word that describes how it makes me feel. I'm heading for the Secret Valley because I'm guessing that's where she lives. It must be somewhere in the Melody Mountains."

"I don't imagine you've ever been out of Spring Gate, so how do you expect to find that valley?"

"I've figured out a method. There's a saying in the Melody Tales that's always fascinated me: "the heart knows the way". I'm going to let my heart be like a guiding star."

Gustafus sat up straight in his chair and looked at Gideon. He was impressed."That's intriguing," said Gideon. "I've done some studies on the heart myself. How exactly are you going to do it?"

"I'm going to hum, like I always do to make things grow better. My mother used to sing to our plants—the flowers, the apple trees. We're noted for having the most colorful flowers and the best tasting apples in the valley and I think that's why. I don't sing songs with words like she did. Aunt Prudence doesn't approve, but I do hum softly and make up tunes for our trees and flowers. They seem to tell me what their melodies might be. And it feels so good when I hum from my heart. After all, according to the Melody Tales the world was created by music and the Magic Singer's song is supposed to be in such perfect harmony that anything or anyone who hears it pops back into tune. Anyway, this is what I plan to do. Once I'm through the gap in the hills I'll stop. Then I'll point myself in one direction and hum. If my heart feels good then I'll go that way. If my heart feels strange then I'll try the same thing in another direction."

"Hmm…interesting, it could work. When are you planning to leave?"

"Not for another month, after the snow melts in the mountain passes."

"Good, we've got lots of time then."

"Thank you. I can tell we're going to be friends. I haven't had a close friend since Amy moved away. Fortunately, she'll be back in a year. If we didn't write each week, I don't know what I'd do. Well, thank you again. I need to get to my chores because this afternoon I'm supposed to help Aunt Violet. That's going to interfere with my studying the Melody Tales. Volume Six has songs to the Magic Singer. I always had trouble making sense of them but it's occurred to me that they might contain some clues on how to find her. I do have a plan for making time but that definitely is my secret."

She was out the door in a jiffy with Fidelity fluttering behind her.

"A friend…like Amy?" said Gideon, when the door closed. "We have a lot of work to do, Gustafus."

Chapter Four

JELLY SONGS

Susanna closed the back door and bustled around the side of the house and said: "I'll be back in time for supper, Aunt Prudence, and I'm wearing my shawl."

Good, she thought, I made it without telling a lie. I will be back before supper. All I have to do is leave Aunt Violet's an hour earlier than Aunt Prudence would expect, and then I'll stop at my favorite spot and study. I'll tell Aunt Violet that since I have some things to do before supper, I'll need to leave in good time. As long as she doesn't ask me what those things are I'll be fine.

She hoisted her bag's strap higher on her shoulder as Fidelity balanced on her other one. Susanna scurried down the path that led through the woods to Amy's house. The path was well worn because of the years of friendship between the two families.

Susanna slowed down to enjoy the woods. The Mansfield's had left the land alone here, so the trees had found their own spots to grow.

Even with her slow steps she didn't see the fairies. All she saw were the sunlit grasses and wildflowers. If she had looked deeper, she would have seen that within the pools of sunlight were colored lights and then if she had looked deeper still, she would have discovered that within the lights stood the little people of beautiful face, form and wing. They were lined up along the path like people along a parade route, staring with wonder. Short ones—well under six inches, tall ones and a few slender twelve-inch tree fairies had left their work to look at Fidelity sitting on Susanna's shoulder.

Their voices chimed together like tiny bells. "Look, look," they said to each other. "She's been assigned to a person! What an honor! How fortunate! Look, she earned the girl who hums."

Fidelity nodded to the left and right, her face pink with happiness. When they reached the field around Amy's house, the voices faded away. Fidelity turned around and gave a wave.

The path led up to the back door of the house. The outside looked like the usual unadorned box from the back but it was built in a 'u' around a courtyard. No one else had a courtyard in Spring Gate. A house was either a square or a rectangle and only a modest sized porch was considered proper—certainly a courtyard wasn't. Ages and ages ago houses were supposed to have been huge with pillars but today no one would dare have one board more than was considered necessary.

Susanna and Amy had spent many moments sitting in the courtyard and staring through the gap in the hills at the Melody Mountains. Amy was the only one she talked to about the Melody Tales. Was the secret valley really there, they would ask each other in whispers? Were there really fairies and gnomes?

Aunt Violet came to the back door when Susanna knocked.

Susanna followed her into the kitchen. "That's a beautiful blue dress you're wearing, Aunt Violet. Do you know what it reminds me of—the color of the sky just after the sun has dipped behind the mountains."

"It's my favorite shade. Sit down, dear. Let's get acquainted."

"I can't remember but are you my mother's older sister or younger sister?"

"Her older sister, dear."

Susanna looked at her aunt's flawless skin, her slender figure and the thick braid falling down her back. "You don't look that old."

"I sing a young tune. It keeps the wrinkles away. I could teach you to sing a song that would carry you all the way to the middle of who you are and retune your every part back into happiness."

"Have you read the Melody Tales, Aunt Violet?"

"Of course, dear. I was raised on them."

"That sounded like something right from one of their pages. The thing is I haven't always understood everything I've read. The volume I like the best is the one that tells the stories from the early days in the Melody Mountains. It's written so simply that I understood it when I was ten years old. Are you going to train me to be a traveling singer, like my mother was? I don't think Aunt Prudence would allow it."

"I want you to be a stay-at-home singer. A song can do a lot if it's repeated over and over in the same place. The power of song is something most people have forgotten and that's why the crops are starting to fail."

Susanna looked intently at her aunt. "Is there magic in singing?"

"Oh yes."

"If I take lessons will I be able to help the drought?"

"Indeed, my dear."

"The Melody Tales say that all life must sing in tune in order for the earth to be rich and full of life...or something like that. Is that what you're talking about?"

"Yes, Susanna. I'm glad you can understand. It makes my task easier. We'll keep the lessons a secret for the moment. Well, do you accept?"

"I guess so. I have trouble remembering my mother's face but I can easily recall her voice. If I could sing like she could I'd be very happy. She had sunshine in her voice."

"Your first lesson is helping me with my jellies. Yes, that's right. I'll bring my latest batch of jellies to the table and then you can do quality control. They're in the pantry. Help me carry them."

After they had assembled fifty jars of jelly on one side of the kitchen table, Aunt Violet brought in her specially designed jelly boxes. She put them on the floor beside Susanna's chair."

"Now dear, put the first jar to your ear and let me know what you hear."

Susanna stared at her aunt and then at the jellies. She picked up the jar and held it to her ear. Maybe Aunt Violet wanted to determine if the wax seal jiggled. If it did then air could get in and the jelly could spoil.

"I didn't hear a thing, Aunt Violet."

"Listen again."

Susanna obliged and put the jelly up to her other ear. She didn't hear a peep but after a minute she let out a sigh.

"Nothing, but I'm feeling quite relaxed."

"Good, that means that you're hearing the jelly's melody."

"There's music in the jelly?"

"Yes dear. "I've learned how to put my song into the jellies. You may have heard there's an herb for every ailment. Well, there's a song for every ailment too and not just ailments of the body but of the thoughts and feelings. The first lesson of singing is learning how to listen. A singer must hear the song before she can sing it. Try this next jar. Pretend you're in the woods and you're listening for a bird's song. It's that kind of listening."

She sat at the kitchen table for an hour but never heard a note.

"I'm becoming very relaxed though," she said to Aunt Violet. "And I've started seeing pretty pictures in my mind and strangely enough, they've been the same color as the jelly I'm listening too."

"That's good," said Aunt Violet. "That's an excellent start. You'll be hearing their songs soon."

"Aunt Violet, you sound like a page out of the Melody Tales. I'm going to enjoy coming here. But I do have to leave now. I…uh, I still have some things to do before supper."

"Of course, dear." She took Susanna's hands in hers as they both stood up. "I hope you enjoyed your first lesson."

She leaned forward and kissed Susanna's cheek and as she did she whispered in a tiny whisper to Fidelity: "Stay."

When Susanna went out the front door Fidelity looked longingly after her.

"Don't worry, Fidelity," said Aunt Violet. "You can catch up with her later. I need to teach you a new song."

Susanna pulled her shawl out of the bag and arranged it on her favorite rock. The flat rock seemed to grow out of the side of the gentle slope. She sat down and opened her book.

"Your aunts think you're at Amy's house," said a voice from higher up the slope.

Susanna turned around. "Gerda," she said. "What are you doing here?"

"Looking for you."

"Why?"

Gerda blushed and looked away. "I want you to leave Burl alone."

Susanna stared, her mind blank.

"Don't look so innocent," said Gerda, facing her with hands rolled into fists. "I know you want him but you can't have him. He promised me we'd be married when he got his ten acres on his birthday." At that she sat down in a heap and burst into tears.

"Gerda, for heavens sake," she said, slipping her book into her bag and standing up. "I don't want Burl. Whatever gave you that idea?"

"You don't?" sniffed Gerda.

"Absolutely, positively not! I've never paid any attention to him so why would you think that?"

"His mother told my mother that Burl was going to get you as a wife. She boasted that only a man like Burl, with a mother like her, would be able to tone you down. She always finds something to brag about to my mom because she hates it that Mom beats her every spring fair in the bread contest. Maybe she thinks winning the contest will make up for her dirty house."

"I'm not going to marry Burl. He's certainly never asked me so why would she say that? Oh dear...they're coming to tea in a few days and Aunt Prudence asked me to be nice to him.

I thought it was strange, because we never have anything to do with them and Mrs. Ringwurst seems to dislike me. Surely she wouldn't accept a marriage between Burl and me?"

"Oh yes she would," said Gerda. "She's very ambitious. You know you're rather ...different and it would be a real feather in her cap if Burl could marry someone like you and tone you down."

"But surely Aunt Prudence wouldn't...she might...she might and say it's for my own good. She's been badgering me lately about blending in. I guess arranging a marriage with someone like Burl, would be her way of helping me. Don't worry Gerda, there's no way I'd ever marry Burl, no matter what Aunt Prudence did."

"What can you do? I love Burl but I know he does whatever his mother tells him. Your aunt could marry you by proxy if you wouldn't co-operate and then lock you out of the house. Remember, that's what happened to Jane Foremost several years ago. She had no choice but to go to her husband's place."

"I don't know what I'm going to do but I'll think of something. See if you can get Burl to stand up to his mother. I'd make him an awful wife."

"You certainly would! I'm the only one who wouldn't nag him, well, maybe a little and only when he really needed it."

Chapter Five

TEA WITH THE RINGWURSTS

Susanna tossed and turned in bed. Maybe she should have confronted Aunt Prudence. No, she thought, her aunt could be resourceful, so it was best to act as if she knew nothing of the betrothal plans. But what could she do? It was too early to go into the mountains. (More tossing and turning.) If only she had some magic then she could make her self invisible. Didn't the Melody Tales say that some people could disappear if they needed to?

Now just a minute! She sat up and pushed the pillow behind her back.

The only reason Erna Ringwurst wanted her was because she was unusual. Well, she would act like an ordinary girl, so ordinary she'd blend right into the tea table. In that way she would become invisible. That was the solution and Aunt Prudence wouldn't be able to do a thing about it.

With that, she plumped her pillow the way she liked it and settled down to sleep.

A couple hours later, Fidelity flew into the room through the closed window. She watched Susanna smiling in her sleep and gave her cheek a whisper of a kiss. Then she stood on the bedside table and began to sing.

Here's a special coat for you,
Woven in a pretty blue.
It will keep you nice and warm,
Sheltered from your auntie's storm.
It is full of Violet's love
And will fit you like a glove.
Never worry, never fear,
Music that you cannot hear,
Helps you chase that awful gloom,
With Aunt Violet's woven tune.

Fidelity sang it once through, wrinkling her forehead as she tried to remember the words. Then she flew to Susanna's pillow and pulled a blue gem from her pocket. After polishing it on her dress she walked around the edge of the bed, singing and shaking the gem like a saltshaker. Blue sparkles soon outlined Susanna's body. Fidelity stopped at the top of the bed but kept singing. Threads of blue came out of the sparkles and wove over and under each other as they covered Susanna. The coat settled into her in a puff of blue and all traces disappeared. She turned in her sleep and let out a relaxed sigh.

Fidelity could hear the song that Susanna heard in her dreams. She curled up beside her on the pillow, and as she pocketed the gem and arranged her dress neatly, she felt Susanna's breath warm her. Soon, she too was fast asleep.

Three afternoons later Susanna walked into Aunt Violet's parlor. Fidelity flew behind her.

"It's hard work listening to those jellies," said Susanna, flopping down on a chair. She was quiet for a few moments and then turned to her aunt. "Where you come from, in Songward, do parents arrange marriages for their children?"

Her aunt counted three more stitches and then laid her knitting on the side table. "No dear, men and women are expected to use their hearts to find the perfect mate. That's a great challenge, but it's considered part of growing up."

"That makes so much sense! I can't remember much of what Mother told me about Songward except it was on the other side of the Melody Mountains and lots of the people were singers. I thought about moving there but I know Aunt Prudence would bring me back."

Susanna watched her pick up her knitting and complete the row. "Aunt Prudence wants to marry me off to Burl Ringwurst. I have a plan though—a good one. The idea came to me a few nights ago before I went to sleep. It all depends on keeping my mouth closed during tomorrow's tea with Erna Ringwurst. I have a feeling I should sew my lips together because Erna could bring out the worst in me. What if it doesn't work? Imagine being part of the Ringwurst family!"

"Let's go outside. I've something to show you."

Susanna and Fidelity followed her to the courtyard. The afternoon sun had warmed the flagstones nicely.

"Aunt Violet!" she said, running to the edge of the courtyard and then down the two steps to the lawn. "This is beautiful. What a wonderful idea to put a mirror here between the two cherry trees. It looks like a door." She looked herself up and down and twirled around. "I've never seen all of me at once before. Aunt Prudence says big mirrors make big heads."

Susanna moved back to the steps and then walked forward watching her reflection. "I guess I really am tall. I was hoping it wasn't true. That's why I'm so clumsy."

"You're not clumsy, dear; you're just in a hurry to experience life. The mirror *is* a door. If you can see beyond your reflection you can walk through it. Now, sit in this chair and close your eyes. Time for your next singing lesson."

Susanna sat in the wicker chair beside her aunt, still watching the mirror.

"Close your eyes. You won't miss a thing. In fact, you can see a wider world with your eyes closed. Now, look at the area where your heart is. It will be dark at first but imagine there's a summer blue sky. Then picture the sun in that sky. Feel the sun's warmth in your heart. The sun is your center. Breathe in slowly, smoothly and as you do see a rainbow flowing into the sun. When you breathe out, the rainbow rolls out of your heart like a happy stream. I call this the heartfire breath. You're creating a path for your voice to travel on. Practice it several times now—threading the rainbow ribbon through your heart as you breathe. Breathe in and the rainbow fills the sun, breathe out and it streams out."

Susanna opened her eyes for an instant to glance at the mirror. Her aunt shook her head. Sitting up straighter, she closed her eyes again. Fidelity sat on her shoulder, eyes closed and forehead wrinkled as she concentrated on doing the lesson. Susanna remembered the rainbow she had seen last summer, the brightest in a while. Shrinking it down with her imagination she let it stream into the sun she pictured in her heart. Then as she breathed out, she imagined it spreading like a pathway before her.

A breeze warmed her face, a summer wind…much too warm for this time of year. Susanna opened her eyes and looked at the trees beyond the courtyard. Not a leaf moved. Still the breeze caressed her face. The mirror no longer reflected the windows of the house. Instead it showed a green field with a hazy, pillared home beyond.

She leapt up, rushed down the steps to the mirror, but just saw her reflection. "This is a magic mirror, isn't it?"

"Yes dear."

"Tell me about it."

"Not yet, dear."

"Aunt Violet!"

"I want you to figure it out by yourself. The lessons I give you should help. Now, I do believe Gideon is in the kitchen delivering my jelly boxes. You can walk home together."

Susanna gazed into the mirror for a few moments and then walked up to the courtyard. She kissed her aunt on the cheek.

"Someday you'll have to teach me some of your magic. I could use it in my present dilemma."

"What makes you think I'm not teaching you magic now?"

"These are magic lessons?"

"That's right. Not all magic is flashy. In fact, the best magic begins gently, then one day you wake up and find it has become a natural part of your life."

"I could use some flashy stuff in the meantime, though."

"Try the heartfire breath, dear. It's quite powerful after you've practiced it for a while. Oh, there you are Gideon. Susanna is ready to leave. Good bye for now." She stood up and walked into the house.

"Gideon, come and have a look at this mirror."

She took hold of his hand and led him down the steps. Gustafus trailed behind. "Walk slowly," she said. "It's fascinating to see yourself walking towards you. Of course, I don't want to become too fascinated, like that man in the Melody Tales who fell in love with his reflection. That's how the whole trouble started apparently. Isn't it strange that people don't believe the Melody Tales yet no one is supposed to have big mirrors. It makes me think that at sometime in the past people did believe. So, what do you see when you look in the mirror?" They stood in front of it, still hand-in-hand.

Gideon and Fidelity chuckled as they watched Gustafus poke his head around Gideon and wiggle his eyebrows.

"People usually see what they expect to see in a mirror," said Gideon.

"You like to talk in riddles don't you? Well, Aunt Violet says it's a magic door." She leaned closer to him and whispered: "I'm going to figure out how to walk through it."

Susanna looked at the mirror intently and then noticed

that Gideon was watching her. They were still holding hands. She released his hand and started walking away. "I need to get my bag from the kitchen, you go ahead, and I'll catch up."

Gideon and Gustafus were waiting for her by the back door when she came out.

"Gideon, do my aunts know you came here?"

"Your Aunt Prudence does. She saw me with the boxes and asked about them. Why?"

"Oh, well…I guess I can trust you. I want to study at my favorite rock before I go home. Could you sneak back to the workshop? If they saw you they might ask you about me and you'd have to tell them, of course. Aunt Prudence wouldn't like it if she knew I was taking a whole hour out of the day to study one of these books."

"I'll stay with you while you study."

"All right, but don't expect me to talk to you."

"I'm fond of silence. Don't worry about me." Gideon said this with a wink at Fidelity and Gustafus.

After a while, they left the path and walked down the slope to Susanna's rock. She settled herself in for studying. Gideon lounged on the grass beside her. She watched him out of the corner of her eye for a few moments. He looked straight ahead and hummed a tune.

What Susanna could not see was the group of fairies in front of him. They were lined up in three rows with Fidelity in the center. Gustafus was the conductor. He cleared his throat, turned his head and when Gideon nodded, he raised his arms. "One, two, let's sing," he said.

The fairies began singing the words to the tune Gideon hummed.

Sing a song of springtime's bloom,
Ripening to harvest soon.
My sweet love sits very near.
Could she, would she ever hear

The song ringing in my heart,
For I've loved her from the start.
In a dream I saw her face,
Full of light and simple grace.
Sing my song of Springtime's bloom,
Ripening to harvest soon.

They repeated the song several times. At first, Susanna studied her book intently, oblivious to her surroundings. Then she lifted her head, thinking she heard something. She glanced at Gideon and then stared as if she'd never seen him before. When she felt herself blushing, she dropped her gaze.

This feels so awkward, she thought. I can't stand it. He feels much too…too…close. She stood up quickly and threw her book into her bag.

"Let's go," she said, without looking at him.

"Sure," he said, standing up and surveying her pink cheeks. He turned towards the fairies and smiled. Gustafus bowed and dismissed the choir.

Susanna rushed up the slope, tripping over a tree root as she tied the ends of her shawl. Gideon put a hand out to steady her but she ignored it.

"I'd better have this shawl on when I get home. Aunt Prudence is always after me to wear it if the air has the slightest coolness. My father and mother died of pneumonia, so she's got it in her head that I'm delicate too. Now she's got me worrying that I'll never live to be a little old lady. Did you start my wheelbarrow today? Every time I've visited you you're always working on something else. I'd like to have it ready as soon as possible, in case I have to leave early."

She chattered nonstop until they met Aunt Maisy coming from the village.

"We've just come from Aunt Violet's," she said and her cheeks flushed pink—again. "Gideon had to deliver some boxes for the jellies, so we walked back together."

"Let me carry those parcels for you, Miss Mansfield," said Gideon.

"Thank you, Gideon. They were getting a mite heavy. I couldn't resist the dark brown sugar Henry had in at the General Store; it'll go so well in my ginger cookies." She looked with interest at Susanna's blushing cheeks.

She grew uncomfortable under her aunt's gaze. "I need to get started on the potatoes," she said, and then she rushed towards the house.

"Gideon," said Aunt Maisy, "about the tea tomorrow afternoon…"

On the afternoon of the tea, Susanna surveyed the dining room table set with her mother's china and silverware. The cutlery with its rose-shaped tops reflected the light but to her, the greatest delight was the shiny plates. She examined each one, making sure it was right side up with the blossoming trees at the top and the spring green grass at the bottom. As she checked, she counted the places…seven! Quickly she counted on her fingers: "Me, Aunt Prudence, Aunt Maisy, Mr. Ringwurst, Mrs. Ringwurst, Burl…that's six." Perhaps Aunt Maisy was flustered when she set the table. Well, she wasn't going to say anything; she had enough to deal with.

Ordinary, ordinary, she chimed in her thoughts, I have to act ordinary. The best thing I can do is keep quiet.

The front door knocker sounded.

She heard Aunt Prudence going to the door, heard her words of welcome and then Erna Ringwurst's voice seized control. That voice seemed to sink into every nook and cranny of her home and Susanna thought it would still bark at her long after the Ringwursts left.

Taking a deep breath she went into the parlor, where Aunt Prudence had ushered her guests. She kept her eyes downcast like she had seen Gerda do at school. That's why she missed the sullen look Burl gave her. But at Erna's first words, her eyes widened.

"Prudence, I refuse to call this gal by that ridiculous long name. She's Sue and that's all she'll get from me. How do you do, Sue."

Erna Ringwurst planted herself in front of Susanna in all her carefully cultivated ordinariness of iron gray hair stretched up into a bun and a dress that did not allow one scrap of lace, ribbon, extra tucks, or anything that would call attention to it.

Fear seized Susanna. She knew she had met someone who might squish every ounce of happiness out of her.

Aunt Prudence took charge. "Now Erna, she would have let me starve her before she'd be called Sue. Isn't that right, Susanna?"

A quick nod was all Susanna could give.

"Susanna," said Aunt Prudence, "you escort Burl into the dining room, Maisy you take Tom, and Erna, you and I can follow."

The strange group shuffled into the dining room.

"Tom," she said, "you sit over there beside Maisy, and Erna, you're beside me at this end. Burl, you're right there beside Susanna. Goodness gracious, Maisy, can't you count, there's one place too many."

A knock sounded at the back door and Maisy whisked off to answer it. Everyone was seated by the time she returned. She led Gideon to the empty chair beside Susanna.

"There," she said, sitting down. "I thought it was appropriate for our new carpenter to share tea with us so he could meet some neighbors." She made the introductions around the table and then stared as defiantly as she could at Prudence.

Aunt Prudence quickly hid her surprise and anger. "Tom," she said, "you start the sandwiches. Burl, you get the pickles going in the other direction."

"Lands sake, Prudence," said Erna, "where did you get these plates. Look at the trees and grass painted on them. I feel like I'm eating on the ground. Plates should be plain, don't you know."

"These belong to Susanna, they were her mother's."

"Trust a traveling singer to have such bizarre china. I certainly wouldn't allow it in my house. Didn't your mother have some fancy name too? Sue, I'm talking to you."

Forget the heartfire breath, Susanna thought, I can barely breathe at all I'm so mad. "Her name was Glorianna," she finally said.

"Glo…ri…an…na," said Erna, counting on her fingers. "Four! That's four syllables. If everyone had such fancy names, we'd use our breath up just calling to each other. I must say, Prudence, your house needs some toning down. But I guess your family has always been odd. Didn't Sue's father have those silly books? They came down through his grandfather, I heard. I never allow such things in my house. You know what I always say—if you want to see how ordinary should look, come to my home. I don't have one fancy thing calling attention to itself. Now, if we became…better acquainted, I'd be willing to help you set your place in proper order." She pushed a dainty sandwich into her mouth and chewed efficiently. Then she fixed her eyes on Gideon. "You there, what's your name again."

"Gideon," he said, turning to Susanna with a wry expression.

"So," said Erna, "you're their hired man."

"He's his own man," snapped Susanna, "He rents my father's workshop. And he makes beautiful cupboards out of incredible wood."

"Uppity miss, isn't she," said Erna, with a significant look at Aunt Prudence.

Oh no, thought Susanna, why didn't I keep my mouth shut.

That tea seemed to go on forever. Susanna clamped her lips together and kept her eyes lowered. She pushed the food around on her plate but seldom took a bite. Both Aunt Maisy and Gideon gave her concerned looks.

When the Ringwursts were finally at the front door saying

their goodbyes, she walked upstairs to her room after a brief nod at the guests. She was exhausted.

Aunt Prudence knocked on her door a few minutes later.

"Susanna," she said, "I agreed to Erna's request that you visit her one day this week."

"Why?" asked Susanna, as she stood up and faced her.

"She wants to become better acquainted with you."

"Are you going to tell me the truth?"

"Susanna," she said, sitting on the bed. "You know I don't like to mention my age, but remember Maisy and I were grown up when your father was born. We're practically old ladies now and when we're gone there won't be anyone to take care of you. You say you don't want to blend in, but if you don't then nobody will associate with you. A person has to have some friends, someone to say hello to now and again. You'd just wither away by yourself. Remember how hard school was for you with just Amy being your friend? Your mother was shunned completely by our neighbors because she refused to blend. She wore those bright clothes, sang her songs all over the place and laughed too much. There's no chance of anyone getting above anyone else if we all act the same. It wasn't too bad for her because she had your father and Maisy and me. But you would have no one and I cannot allow that to happen. So, I've offered your hand to Burl, and Erna is thinking about it. She'd like to look you over some more to see if you'll suit her son. You must do this. Your future depends on it."

Susanna went over to her window and looked out for a moment. Then she turned to her aunt. "I can't believe you'd give me to that woman. How could you do such a thing? Don't you love me?"

"It's because I love you that I'm doing it."

"Oh, Aunt Prudence, that can't be love to put me under Erna Ringwurst's thumb. She can't wait to squish me."

Aunt Prudence stood up and walked to the door. "Love has to sacrifice, Susanna and that's what I'm doing. You will obey me."

"Never! I will not go over to that woman's home and I will certainly not marry Burl."

"Oh yes you will. You will go over to Erna's in four days. You will go over after breakfast and return before supper. If you don't obey me I shall burn your books."

At that parting shot, Aunt Prudence left the room. Susanna rushed to her dresser and pulled open the top drawer. Her books were gone.

Chapter
Six

SUSANNA WANTS TO ESCAPE

The rays of the early morning sun slanted through the apple trees as Fidelity led Gideon through the orchard. Susanna sat on the broken pillar beside the big fir. Her eyes stared, unseeing, into the woods beyond. Gideon sat beside her and took her hand. She stiffened for a moment then burst into tears.

He said nothing, even when her sobs stopped. Soon she sat taller and dried her eyes.

They sat quietly for a few more minutes and then Gideon stood and pulled her up. "Come on, I'll show you what I made for you. No, it's not the wheelbarrow. I can make that in a day, so there's no hurry. Let's go and you can tell me why you're upset."

Once they were inside the shop, he led her to the workbench by the window. A remarkable little bookshelf sat on top with its purple wood shining in the light. Swirls of trailing flowers painted with gold were etched into its top and sides. The front had double doors of framed glass latched with a golden lock and key.

"This is yours," he said, "made to measure for the seven volumes of your Melody Tales."

"It's beautiful but you're too late, I don't have them anymore. Aunt Prudence…stole them from my top drawer and she'll burn them unless I marry Burl."

Susanna went on to tell him everything about Aunt Prudence's plan.

"I'm not going to give in," she finished, "she can burn my books but I still won't do it. It feels like everything has been taken from me. My home doesn't feel safe anymore. Thinking about that beautiful singer made my life sparkle but now all I can think of is escaping this wretched future. Maybe Aunt Violet can help me, but if she can't, then I'll want that wheelbarrow. You don't have any solutions, do you?"

Gideon looked at her for the longest time as if he wanted to say something but then he shook his head.

"Somehow I think you're supposed to stay put and solve the problem. Problems can follow you wherever you go."

"If I have to stay here then Aunt Violet had best give me some special magic. I'd better get going. She should be up by now."

Gideon let her leave. From the workshop window he watched her take the path that led to Violet's.

"Gustafus," he said, "I want you to go on a treasure hunt for me. You'll be looking for seven books with blue leather binding and gold lettering."

Susanna walked into the kitchen of her aunt's house.

"Aunt Violet, where are you? I need you."

"In the dining room," called Aunt Violet.

She was sitting at the dining room table. The morning light picked out the tablecloth's rainbow glints.

"Sit down, dear," she said, "and tell me why you're here so early."

"Aunt Violet, I need magic—strong magic. If you could make the Ringwursts disappear I'd be mighty grateful. Not forever, of course, a few months should do it. If you can't do that, then teach *me* to disappear. I have to escape."

"Escape what, dear?" asked Aunt Violet.

"Aunt Prudence and Erna Ringwurst." For the second time that morning Susanna told her story.

Aunt Violet patted her hand when she finished. "Don't

worry, there's a solution. I can give you a push in the right direction."

"What direction might that be?"

"A new direction—the very center of north, south, east and west."

"As long as Erna isn't there, I'll be satisfied."

Aunt Violet laughed. "You know, your mother had that same sense of humor. Even in a tight corner she could come up with a joke."

She reached across the table and took Susanna's hand. "I'll show you how to escape. Inside of everyone is a secret room that is the entrance to a marvelous world. Within the room are musical solutions to every problem. This first time I'll lead you there, but next time you'll have to find it yourself. Close your eyes, dear. Relax yourself with the heartfire breath and listen to my song."

"All right," said Susanna, "I'll play along. I would rather have some flashy magic but then, nobody seems to do what I think they should."

Violet hummed a melody with notes that glided together so smoothly Susanna felt she was floating on them.

She was dreaming, she thought, as she strolled beside her aunt. They moved along a sky blue path created by the melody. Ahead of them shone one light like a star. Then a brown fog spread before them and as they moved through the fog she could see a tangle of dusty brambles across their pathway. The brambles shivered with a droning tune and each vibration shook more dust into the air.

Her aunt smiled and took her hand. They started to pass through the tangled growth. Nothing touched her, but she heard. Each withered twig droned with her familiar thoughts, the ones that lurked in the background of her mind. Some were boring, some anxious, some angry and resentful.

"Stop listening to them," said Aunt Violet.

Soon they passed the brambles and were in a place of

fragrant trees and shrubs. Soft grass welcomed her feet. This too rang with music, but with the delightful tunes of her happy thoughts, the ones that always cheered her up.

At the edge of the lawn stood a building with walls so white, she had to squint. Aunt Violet ushered her through the open door. The room sang. Every part of it chimed with music—the walls, the floor, the pink velvet chair, the window and its gossamer curtains fluttering in a breeze, the breeze itself, and the beautiful flower in a white bowl on the table before the chair.

Aunt Violet told her that this was her room. She was simply her guest. The pink chair was made just for her.

As she settled down into its velvet plushness, she observed the flower before her. It looked alive with flame-like white petals dancing in the rhythm of the breeze.

The flower opened its petals and revealed a diamond in its center. Each facet of the diamond was a window she could gaze into. Her eye was drawn to one and in an instant she was looking through it at a life-size scene. It was her home, but different, as if it had been washed with new sunshine. Susanna felt that nothing could harm the peace that glowed from it—nothing would want to. She heard children singing inside the house and then she recognized her own voice—rising above yet blending with their song. Her voice sounded different—richer, reaching the high notes with ease. A man's voice joined them and its deepness cradled all their voices. That voice was so familiar. It almost sounded like…

"We must go back now," spoke her aunt's thoughts to her. "Remember this always. It shows what your future will be if you follow the song in your heart. Remember…remember…to follow that song."

Susanna raised her head and opened her eyes. She was still sitting at the dining room table. Aunt Violet had brought in the tea tray. She saw the steam curling up from the cups and smelled the flowery tea blend. The cup gently rocked in its saucer as Aunt Violet placed it in front of her.

"Aunt Violet," she said, marveling at how relaxed her voice sounded, "Where you took me was amazing, wonderful...but how can it save me from having to marry Burl?"

"You saw a picture of your future. Now, tell me, did you hear or see any of the Ringwursts?"

"No."

"Did you see their house or land?"

"I only saw my home looking much nicer."

"You know if you married Burl you would not be living at home, so obviously he is not your intended."

"How can that picture give me my future?"

"People have forgotten they are composers. We compose music with every thought and feeling and our life is created according to the music we play. If we don't like our life then we must change our tune. That means going inside to the music room and finding the perfect picture for each part of our life. With the picture comes the music that waltzes it into creation. If you keep your attention on the picture and listen for its song, the music will entice your outer life to flow into the patterns of that picture. It's easy to remember this now, but later it will fade and you'll wonder if you really saw or heard any of this. Quiet yourself with the breath and the memory will return to refresh you. Now, have a good cup of tea before you go back."

Susanna stretched in her chair and Fidelity, who had been watching from the windowsill, fluttered to her shoulder. Susanna blinked, then sat up straight and looked around.

"My goodness," she said, "For a moment I thought I saw a...a hummingbird fly over to me. That dream is making me see things. I definitely need a cup of tea."

She walked slowly back home after leaving Aunt Violet's. Before she reached her favorite rock, her dream adventure started fading. It was as if something had shut a door over the entrance to the memory. Then the door disappeared behind the backdrop of her regular thoughts and feelings. Again she thought of Aunt Prudence and the Ringwursts and the old worries descended.

When she walked into the kitchen, only Aunt Maisy was there. Susanna cut herself a slice of bread and joined her aunt at the table.

"Susanna," whispered Aunt Maisy. "I agree you should get married so someone can look after you when we're gone, but not Burl. Erna comes with Burl and she'd sour any milk she looked at. Do you know, Tom Ringwurst used to be a pleasant sort of man before he married her. You could always count on him for a smile when you saw him in the village. Now it hurts my heart to see him, he looks so whipped. I don't know what I can do to help you but I'm thinking, I'm thinking. Don't give up hope. There has to be a solution. How about Violet? Maybe she can think of something."

"She's trying to help me, but I don't know if what she's taught me can change things."

"Susanna," shouted Aunt Prudence, from the parlor, "come in here right now."

"Just humor her for a while," whispered Aunt Maisy. "We'll think of something. Whatever you do, don't back her into a corner or she'll get real ornery. Go on, you'd better get in there and I'd better check the hen house."

"Yes, Aunt Prudence?" said Susanna, as she walked into the parlor.

Her aunt was busy putting wood on the fire and didn't look up. "I want a fire in here all day, that's your job. These chairs and cushions need a good drying. Our winter has been too damp and I will not let things go mildewy."

She straightened up but avoided looking at Susanna. "You can bring in some more wood as you need to."

As Aunt Prudence bustled towards the door she almost bumped into Gideon. She gasped and put her hand to her heart. He carried the volumes of the Melody Tales in one arm and the bookcase in the other.

"Susanna," he said, walking up to the table against the window and putting down the books and the case. "I know you don't like your aunt to see these books, but surely you didn't have to hide them under the potatoes in the root cellar. They could get moldy."

"How in the world?" sputtered Aunt Prudence. "You… you…how dare you!"

Gideon ignored her and opened the case to put the books inside. He turned the golden key in the lock and then went over to Susanna. "Here" he said, handing her the key, "they're safe now."

He walked out of the parlor, nodding to Aunt Prudence as he passed her.

Aunt Prudence stormed over to the table. "Give me the key, Susanna."

Susanna looked down at the tiny key in her hand. "No," she said, as her fingers closed over it.

Lunging for the case, Aunt Prudence picked it up and rushed over to the fireplace.

I will not wrestle with her, Susanna thought; she's only trying to scare me.

"This is your last chance," said Aunt Prudence, holding the bookcase in front of the fire. "Obey me at once."

"You're no better than a thief. I'll never give you this key and I'll never become a Ringwurst. And that's the truth!"

Aunt Prudence heaved the bookcase on top of the fire.

"No!" screamed Susanna, as she leaped towards the fireplace.

"Don't, you silly girl," said Aunt Prudence, wrapping her arms around her shoulders and pulling her back. "Do you want to get burned?"

Her eyes wide with horror, Susanna watched the bookcase. It sat on top of the wood like an unassailable fortress. The flames cradled it but they did not burn it. Neither woman saw beyond the outer shapes of the fire to the dancing flame fairies.

The fairies were dressed in the fire. Their long flickering hair blended with their slender shapes that bent and swayed in time to the song ringing from the bookcase.

Do not burn and do not harm,
Let your forms of flame just charm.
Cool your tiny dancing feet,
Touch not the wood with your heat.
Listen, listen, dance and sway
To the music's cooling way.
You are lovely, soft and sweet,
Cooling flames, fast and fleet.
Magic sings within this wood,
Changing all harm into good.

Susanna broke loose from Aunt Prudence. She reached into the fire and grabbed the bookcase.

"Susanna!" screamed Aunt Prudence.

Only after she had placed the bookcase on the table did she realize she had felt no pain from the fire. She looked at her hands as Aunt Prudence reached her side. They both watched as she turned her hands over. They were unharmed. Not even the sleeves of her blouse were singed. The wood of the bookcase shone as clean and richly purple as ever and not a smudge blackened the glass.

As the diamond-like panes glittered with rainbow lights Susanna remembered her music room. She laughed. I'm going to be all right, she thought. If both I and my beloved books can survive a fire then I'll be safe from Erna…somehow…I can believe it now.

Fidelity and Gustafus giggled together in the hall outside the parlor.

"I'm the one who found the books," said Gustafus, straightening his shoulders and puffing out his chest.

"That's wonderful," said Fidelity. "My Susanna almost saw

me today. I can hardly wait until she really notices me. Then we can become true friends, like you and Gideon."

The two of them stuck their heads around the doorway and watched Susanna and Aunt Prudence. Both women were still staring at the bookcase.

Then Aunt Prudence moved wearily to the chair by the fire and sat down. Susanna looked at her tired face and all of a sudden she understood.

"Aunt Prudence," she said, going to her side and kneeling by her chair. "You don't need to worry about me, about my future. Look at those books I love so much—they're untouched. And you've seen my hands. Surely that should convince both of us that I'll be all right. Try to believe that."

Her aunt raised her eyes to hers. "You're right," she said. "Please forgive me." She leaned back in the chair. "Through all the generations of Mansfield's, there has always been someone who treasured those books. My grandfather, my father, your father—they were always quoting from them. They even believed in such things as fairies. I confess I laughed behind their backs and I was ashamed of them in public. It cost me a lot of effort but I managed to make people accept me in spite of those books. Maisy and I are excellent housekeepers and that has helped, of course. But now I don't know...I just don't know. When I saw your hands and that bookcase, I remembered a line from the tales your father often referred to: "The song protects you from all harm. It even cools fire with its charm." My, I used to smirk at that one. But there may be more to this world than I know. You're right, my dear, somehow there's a better plan for your future than Burl Ringwurst."

Susanna kissed her cheek. Then gently she pressed her own cheek against the spot. "Thank you," she said. "I love you."

Aunt Prudence wrapped her arms around her and held her close.

"Well," she said, patting Susanna's back. "I had best go over to Erna's and tell her the news. Maisy must come with me because I don't think I can handle Erna all by myself. You go and put those books on top of your bureau. And who is this Gideon fellow anyway, that he could make such a case?" She stood up and shook the wrinkles out of her skirt. "I'll deal with that mystery another time. Erna will be enough for one day."

Chapter
Seven

AUNT PRUDENCE CONFESSES AND SUSANNA PROPOSES

Prudence and Maisy took themselves over to the Ringwursts just before lunch time. They reasoned they could honestly tell Erna they needed to be home for the noon meal and thereby have a short visit.

Susanna hummed through the rest of the morning. She hummed to her tulips and narcissus, she hummed to the mushroom and nut casserole she slipped in the oven, and she hummed through the apple orchard touching the blossoms gently with her fingers.

When she knocked on the workshop's door and went inside, she found no one there. She was sure she had heard the sound of a plane scraping on wood. Fresh shavings covered a small workbench but Gideon wasn't there. She wanted to thank him for recovering the books and tell him how wonderful everything was now.

The casserole was ready to be served when she returned to the kitchen but there was no sign of her aunts. She wondered whether she dare prepare the tea. Aunt Prudence liked hers piping hot.

The kettle had begun to boil when her aunts came in the back door. Instantly she knew something was wrong. Aunt Prudence's shoulders slumped and her eyes were red. Maisy guided her sister through the kitchen.

"Come into the parlor, dear," she said over her shoulder. "Bring some strong tea."

Maisy had rekindled the fire in the grate and settled Prudence into the easy chair by the time Susanna came in with the tea. She fixed her sister's tea with lots of sugar and handed it to her. The cup rattled on its saucer as Prudence took it.

"Sit down, Susanna," said Aunt Maisy, settling into her chair. "Our visit was exceedingly strange. I must say I still don't understand what's going on." She looked at Prudence. "Erna insists that you marry Burl but we won't make you, of course. We both are firm about that. But you need to know what Erna plans to tell people if you don't marry her son."

Susanna curled her legs under her as she sat on the sofa. She couldn't take her eyes off Aunt Prudence. When had she ever seen her aunt so upset?

"Let me tell her, Maisy," she said. "I'm the one who knows or rather knows the most." She took a gulp of tea. "Susanna, you know your mother and father died of pneumonia." Aunt Prudence's tea sloshed into the saucer as she hurriedly set it down. "No...no...I'll be fine," she said as Maisy started to get up. "You saw them, I saw them and Maisy saw them. Maisy and I prepared both their bodies for burial. Didn't we, Maisy?"

"Of course, so what is Erna talking about and why are you so upset?"

Aunt Prudence reached for her tea and gulped it down. Maisy immediately prepared her a fresh cup. Susanna stared, unable to think. What was coming?

"Two men from the village helped take the coffins over to our family burial plot," continued Aunt Prudence. "They were to come back later and put the coffins in the ground for us. We had a very nice ceremony. You remember don't you, dear?"

"Yes, of course, I remember. How could I forget," said Susanna, as the memory came back to her. She was seeing again the dancing wind blowing the yellowed grass around the graves. And that almost forgotten memory when a faint perfume of violets swirled around her with a melody that touched her heart and eased her pain.

"We had come back to the house," said Aunt Prudence. "You went up to your room and I looked for those books your father had left you. I couldn't find them so I asked Maisy. She had put them in your father's coffin!"

"You never told me he had asked you to give them to Susanna."

"I know, I know. So, I went back to the graves, by myself. I took a crow bar so I could pry open the coffin to get the books. I opened the coffin and…and…" Aunt Prudence looked at Maisy.

"And what?" she said. "Surely Erna was mistaken."

"No, no, she wasn't. It's true what she said. The bodies were gone. Both of them. I checked. Only the books were there."

"What…what!" stammered Susanna.

"Why didn't you tell me for heavens sakes?" said Maisy, sitting on the edge of her chair. "I'm your sister! What a thing to keep to yourself. How could they be gone?"

"I don't know. I thought I was going crazy for a moment. The nails were still in both of the coffins before I pried them open. I'm sure no one could have opened them. I searched the woods. Nothing! It was so strange. I did the only thing I could think of to do. I filled the coffins with enough dirt to make them heavy and then I nailed them shut. The men came only a few minutes later and I saw them lowered into the ground and buried."

"Why didn't you tell me?" demanded Aunt Maisy. "We could have had some men search the woods more thoroughly."

"And have everyone know their bodies were missing? People always thought we were an unusual family. If they knew this there's no telling how they'd treat us. I did what I had to do to preserve our reputation."

"Aunt Prudence," said Susanna, "How does Erna know this?"

"That Erna," said Aunt Maisy, "she's always been one for

snooping and then using things against people, just to get her own way. Most folks are afraid *not* to be friends with her."

Susanna barely heard Aunt Maisy. She continued to look at Aunt Prudence.

Aunt Prudence leaned her head back against the chair and her eyes filled with tears. "Erna saw the whole thing. There she was hiding behind a tree. And when I was frantically searching in the woods, she went up to the open coffins. She was back hiding again when I shoveled the dirt into them. She's threatening to tell everyone if you don't marry Burl."

"This is the strangest thing I've ever heard," Susanna said as she uncurled her legs and went over to her aunt. She picked up the small stool from the hearth and set it beside the chair. Sitting down, she took her aunt's hand and held it to her cheek.

"I remember seeing mother and father in their coffins. I wanted them to be alive. I wanted them to breathe, but they were so quiet and their hands so cold to touch. But you know, there could be some good explanation. In the Melody Tales, some people never died at all, they just sang a song and then followed that song into a new land, or something like that."

"Please Susanna; I don't want to hear anything about those books."

"Well, I don't see a big problem. It would just be Erna's word against yours."

"She said she'd demand that the mayor have the graves dug up and the coffins opened."

The fire snapped in the grate. Susanna still held her aunt's hand.

"Would it be so very bad if people knew this?" she asked.

"Yes, it would. They think us strange now, but at least they talk to us and buy things from us. We're still a part of the community. But if they decided to shun us we'd have no life at all. Once Maisy and I were gone you'd just wither away by yourself. But...but...oh my dear, I can't let you marry Burl. I can't! Erna would make your life unbearable. You'd be her slave. But I don't know what to do."

"Well, there has to be a solution," said Susanna, standing up. "It makes me furious! We won't let Erna win. We can beat her. Yes, we can. We've got people with magic—Aunt Violet and Gideon. We've even got me. I'm learning things. Listen. This is what we'll do. I'll go over to her place for a day, like she wants, and act as if we're going to knuckle under. This will allow us some time to figure out how to stop her. After all, I can't be married until after my birthday, so that gives us another month. I'm off to Aunt Violet's. Don't worry; we'll get ourselves out of this mess. And don't worry about Mother and Father. It's a mystery about their bodies but I just feel in my heart that they're all right."

She kissed both her aunts and whisked out the door.

Susanna strode down the path to Aunt Violet's. She stubbed her toe twice on tree roots but that did not interrupt her thoughts.

There's supposed to be a world inside me that has the musical answers for problems, she thought. Well, it will have to be a blast of a song to get rid of Erna's meanness. Why did these problems appear just when I decided to go on a quest?

When she walked into her aunt's house she found a note on the kitchen table. "Susanna, make yourself at home," it said. "I'll be back shortly."

The stones on the courtyard floor were turning warm from the afternoon's sun. She sat down on the top step and faced towards the mirror.

It looks like a giant had cut out the side of a huge diamond, she thought, and polished it so he could see his reflection. Could I find my music room by myself and then find the same doorway in my diamond?

She closed her eyes and began the heartfire breath. Rainbow ribbon out and rainbow ribbon in, she said to herself, as she watched her breath.

The dried out brambles appeared. She could hear their droning sound. It was out of tune in a familiar, almost fascinating way—like a story that promised a bizarre revelation. Surely it couldn't hurt to listen for a moment. She'd look for her music room in a minute or two.

She leaned closer to the brambles. The tune made her tired. It seemed to take something from her.

"Listen to me," said the tune, "and I will tell you all about your life. I will take you to the dark places of your mind and show you what is hiding there. Come with me, come with me. I'm an important part of your life. Listen to me! You cannot live without knowing what I will show you."

Susanna did not want to know and yet she did. Anxiety laced its way into her feelings but she wanted to know just a little more and then she'd look for the music room.

She found herself tracing one throbbing bramble with her finger. It was the one that droned the tune. The other brambles seemed to grow from it, as if it was the trunk and the others were branches and twigs and curling tendrils.

Then the tune crashed upon her in a crescendo of fear. No! She did not want to know what was in the dark corners of her mind. Definitely not!

"You can't get away," droned the tune, "I've got you."

A tendril fastened around her wrist and a branch slithered on the ground before her, its twigs and tendrils reaching for her.

"No!" she cried as she tried to break away. The tendril curled and curled around her wrist. The branch came closer.

"Look," droned the tune, "look, I'll force you to see what you don't want to see. You can't escape it."

Susanna looked away from the brambles, trying to see if there was a way to escape. She saw a still, quiet place within her heart—like the eye of a storm. As she looked at the place a slender ribbon of thought wafted in, like a morning sunbeam.

"It's just like a plant," said the thought. "Hum to it."

Susanna cleared her throat and tried to hum. Nothing.

"Close your eyes and pretend it's a rose," said the thought.

I can't close my eyes on the brambles, she thought. It will get me.

"Try it," said the thought. "What else do you know how to do?"

She closed her eyes and pictured the new rose bush she was grooming for the fair. A soft hum came through her lips. Soon she was finding the notes of a melody. When she opened her eyes the melody's ribbon of blue swirled around the tendril. The tendril quivered and grew limp.

Susanna shook it from her wrist.

"Keep humming," said the thought. "Picture the rose."

She did.

When she finally opened her eyes the brambles had disappeared.

Her music room was before her. The door was open so she sat down on her pink chair.

Susanna gazed into the flower on the table before her and the petals opened to reveal their diamond heart. Somewhere in that diamond, she mused, there's a facet that holds the picture and the song I can use to save my family. Her eyes fastened on one near the top of the gem and as she watched, it became larger, like a picture window.

Slowly she stood up, marveling that she felt so light, as if she were barely tethered to the ground. The window became a doorway and through it she saw a house unlike any house she'd ever seen. It was stately and grand with pillars and large windows. For a moment she wondered if it was one of the palatial homes from Spring Gate's past when people had first settled there.

Through the doorway came a tune, sweet and enticing. Susanna stepped over the diamond's threshold and the song grew louder. She walked across a lawn up to the house. Three stories were visible and if it was taller, then those floors were hidden in the white cloud that hung over them like a mist hugging a mountaintop.

The melody seemed louder within the house. Inside, the main hallway was bigger than any parlor in Spring Gate. The dried leaves of many autumns had found homes in the corners. When she looked up, expecting to see a light hanging from a ceiling, she saw there was no ceiling, only light shining through the dust motes as if somewhere, many stories higher, was a window in the roof. The melody came from above.

Susanna climbed the wide curved staircase that led to the second floor. A sturdy railing formed one side of the hall and on the other side were closed doors with mirrors between them. At first, they only reflected her image. But the one right before the stair to the third floor was different. She found herself looking into Erna Ringwurst's bedroom. One stubby candle stood on the faded whitewashed dresser. Erna sat before it brushing her hair while her husband stood behind her.

"Eighty-nine, ninety, ninety-one," she said in time to her brush strokes, "now you listen to me Tom Ringwurst, I'm determined to be the most ordinary person in Spring Gate. Ninety-two, ninety-three, ninety-four. I want to be extra ordinary, so I'll be looked up to. Ninety-five, ninety-six, ninety-seven. That Sue is going to set me on top. Mind you, I'll have to get on top of her to do it. If I can't win the bread making contest, at least I can tame Sue. *And* I'll have one of those finicky Mansfield women to keep my house clean."

"Erna, dear," said Tom, "I…I…I promised Burl he could have the northeast ten acres on his birthday. Uh…dear…he has…someone else in mind for a wife."

"Well, you can unpromise him. I have bigger plans for him. He stays here, with us, so Sue can be right under my nose. Who else do you think has the skill to tone her down? If I left those two alone, she'd be changing him. Ninety-eight, ninety-nine, one hundred and one hundred and one."

Susanna turned away and followed the melody up to the third floor. Mirrors again hung on the walls between the closed doors, but the wooden doors gleamed with polish and the mirrors looked squeaky clean.

Again, just before the stairway to the next floor was a window. This time she looked through it and saw a room that looked like the Ringwurst's bedroom only brighter and warmer. The dresser was now painted and skirted with peach colored silk. Candles spread their light from the corners of the bedroom. Erna sat before her dresser—a younger looking Erna with the fretful lines on her face gone. Her brown hair flowed down her back and a happy Tom Ringwurst stood behind her gently brushing it.

"I swear," said Erna, "when you brush my hair, I lose count. What were you saying about Burl, dear?"

"He just had his coming-of-age birthday. Let's give him the northeast ten acres. He fancies Gerda. You know, the Thompson's youngest girl? She's got enough spunk to make him stand up straight but not too much so she'd bowl him over. What do you think?"

"Gerda, of course. Seems like a good fit to me. Let's tell him tomorrow at breakfast."

Beautiful music came from higher up so Susanna left the Ringwurst's window to climb the steps. The music seemed to tell her she would find something wonderful that she had always wanted.

As she put her foot on the first step she thought about her shawl—was she wearing it? It could be cold up higher. As she looked down, the steps, the house and the music disappeared.

She opened her eyes and saw she was still sitting on the courtyard steps. A rocking chair gently creaked beside her. Aunt Violet sat there knitting, but not as Susanna had usually seen her. Her yarn came from circular skeins of colored light floating a few feet above her. She sang a wordless melody and each note was a color. As the note sounded, a strand of color rippled down and she knitted it into the garment hanging from the silver needles in her lap.

Her aunt smiled at her. "Your eyes are still fresh, like early morning freshness before the world has woken. That's why you can see this." She gestured to the skeins above her head. "My store of magic yarn. Do you like the picture I've sung into this shawl?"

She lifted her needles so Susanna could see the entire knitted triangle.

"It's my home, the one I saw in the diamond's window when you led me to my music room."

"This shawl is for you. Let me tone it down."

She sang the same melody but in a lower octave. The colors dimmed until Susanna only saw flecks of their beauty amidst the white background.

"It disappeared," she said.

"Yes, but it's still ringing with your song, dear. I'm replacing that shawl of worry your Aunt Prudence makes you wear. This shawl holds the picture of your happy future." Her needles flashed as she started casting off.

"Aunt Violet, I made it through the mirror. I saw two Tom and Ernas. The first time they were just like they are now but the second time they were happier and nicer. I don't think I was seeing them when they were younger because they talked about Burl getting married, so it had to be the present time. Why did they seem to have two selves?"

"They have only one self, like all of us. The second time you saw them you would have seen their real self."

"Do you mean that nasty self of Erna isn't real?"

"Yes I do, dear. People let gloomy thoughts and feelings weave a shabby garment around them and then they start believing that shabbiness is who they are. They get other people believing it too."

"If I could talk to Erna's real self then I wouldn't have to worry about being married off to Burl. How could I do that?"

"Excellent question!" said Aunt Violet, casting off the last stitch and then cutting the yarn with her scissors. The skeins above her disappeared. "Underneath the shabby coats are the ribbons of music that compose our song coat—our true garment.

"So I saw Erna and Tom in their song coats? Is that why they looked younger and happier?"

"Yes."

"They thought Gerda would be a good wife for Burl. Somehow I need to get them to take off their old coats."

"Exactly. Open your heart and listen for your magic song. It will fill your heart and spill over into what you say and think. This song is like a warm sun they'll bask in and eventually they'll take off their coats."

"How do I get the song into my speaking voice, if I'm not singing?"

"Words are not big enough or delicate enough to hold all the shades of the song. But your feelings, the ones in your heart, can carry the song into your words. They can fill the words of your everyday speech and the words of your thoughts. So, when you speak, let your voice dip into your heart and gently scoop up that magic."

Susanna stood up and started humming. "I love to hum from my heart. It tickles sometimes, a nice tickle. Will this really work?"

"I promise that if you can sing your song full-hearted, into the teeth of everything that looks gloomy and fearful, you can change the gloom into love. Love is the fiber that holds all life together. The song strums those fibers and as they ripple with the music they shake off their gloomy coats." Aunt Violet stood up and wrapped the shawl around Susanna's shoulders. "Time to go. I've given you all the help I can for now."

Susanna ambled down the path. She wanted time to think before she arrived home. In Aunt Violet's presence it all sounded so easy but now she began to have doubts.

I must make Erna take off her mean coat, she thought, and I have to do it quickly. My birthday is in a month and by then, the snow in the mountain passes should have melted. What if I don't succeed before my birthday? I don't think I could go on my quest and leave Aunt Prudence and Aunt Maisy to the mercy of Erna. Would marrying Burl be the only solution?

As Susanna sank into gloomy thoughts of marrying Burl and living with Erna, Fidelity flew in front of her. She hovered before her face. "Notice me!" she demanded in her tiny voice. "Notice me! I can help. I'm little but I'm big on helping."

Susanna lifted her head. What a sweet breeze, she thought, as she gazed at the treetops. Oh well, maybe I'm worrying over nothing and everything will be much simpler than I imagine.

Chapter
Eight

ERNA'S COAT

Susanna had tossed and turned all night, waking every hour to check the progress of the morning through her window. When the light finally turned bright enough to get up, she felt exhausted. This is not a good start, she told herself. I need all my strength.

Breakfast was a strained affair. Aunt Prudence tried hard to be cheerful, which was uncharacteristic of her and Aunt Maisy sighed after every bite of toast.

Susanna tied her new shawl and rubbed one end against her cheek, hoping to draw courage from it. She opened the back door and turned to her aunts.

"Well, I'll see you just before supper. If I'm not back by then you'll know that Erna served me up for her evening meal."

"Please don't joke like that," said Aunt Prudence. "You're making a sacrifice of yourself...and..." She sniffed as her eyes filled up with tears.

Susanna gave her a long hug. "The only thing I'm sacrificing is a good lunch." Then she kissed Aunt Maisy's cold cheek and went out the door.

Gideon and Gustafus waited for her at the start of the path to the village.

"I thought you might like company on your walk to the Ringwursts," he said as he fell into step beside her. "By the way, why do you allow Erna to order you about?"

Susanna looked at him and wondered what he would think if she told him the story of the empty coffins. He had found her books so maybe he could find out what happened to her mother and father. But she couldn't tell him because fear grabbed her stomach when she thought about death.

"Well," she said, "She can be so mean if someone doesn't do what she wants. So I'm going to pretend to be agreeable until I can figure out a plan to...to make her leave us alone. I'm a little nervous this morning. Maybe if I hum I'll feel better."

"You need a band playing a marching song, like the sort that's played when a hero goes on her way to perform a great deed."

"A day at Erna's doesn't reach that high a level."

Gideon turned his head to wink at the lines of fairies marching along the path's edges. On one side marched the band with their small trumpets, fiddles, flutes and drums, while on the other side marched the choir. Gustafus directed them as he strode ahead of Gideon and Susanna. The choir sang with Fidelity's voice rising above them.

Here the conquering hero comes,
Singing always her sweet hum.
It's the power that can change,
Everything within its range
Into notes of springtime's bliss,
With its gentle, sweetest kiss.
Follow the trail of its sound,
And the magic will be found.
When she finds that perfect blend,
Her old world she will transcend.
Lightly, lightly step and bow,
We all wish her well right now.

The fairy chorus and band stopped where the woods ended and the village began. Spring Gate's homes edged the large meadow. The meadow was like the hub of a wheel and each home's property fanned out like spokes behind the houses in wider and wider spaces until it reached the boundary of Sharpsmere Forest. Only the houses of Aunt Violet and the Mansfield's dared to stay back from the edge of the meadow and hide themselves behind some trees. Erna's house sat at the farther side of the meadow from where Susanna and Gideon stood.

Without realizing it, Susanna slipped her hand in Gideon's as they walked across the meadow.

They finally stood before the Ringwurst's two-story box. A tiny overhang was begrudged to the eaves and a tin roof dared to cover the front steps. The door opened and Erna filled the doorway. When she gazed at Susanna a gloating smile broke out. It reversed itself when she noticed Gideon holding her hand.

"Let go of her!" she thundered. "How dare you touch my prospective daughter-in-law! Sue, you get in here. The breakfast dishes are waiting for you."

Gideon turned to face Susanna and blocked Erna from her view. She felt the sheltering warmth as his other hand covered hers. "I'll be waiting at the edge of your woods. If anything goes wrong just run out the front door. I'll be with you in a flash." He let go of her hand, turned to face Erna and folded his arms in front of him.

Susanna walked towards the house.

"Good morning, Mrs. Ringwurst," she said. "We had better get this settled right now. My name is and always will be Susanna." She stepped into the house and passed Erna.

"Sue Ringwurst it will be when you're married, dearie. I'll not waste my breath over your precious syllables. The kitchen is through there."

Erna pointed straight ahead to the end of the bare entrance hall. Susanna decided to do the dishes rather than fight over her name. She would save her strength for bigger battles.

She whizzed through the dishes and only when she was drying them on a faded tea towel did she look around more closely. It was true. Erna wasn't much of a housekeeper. Dusty cobwebs trailed along the tops of the open shelf above the sink and draped from the top of the curtainless window to the kitchen hutch that leaned into the corner.

"There's no need to turn up your nose at my kitchen," said Erna from the doorway. "I've more important things to do than housework."

Like snooping on your neighbors, Susanna thought to herself.

Erna folded her arms and leaned against the doorframe. "I have a job that will tone you down, dearie. Have you ever changed a feather mattress?"

"Of course," said Susanna.

"Well trained by Prudence, aren't you. I do things differently here. I never throw out the feathers—I wash them and use them again. That's your job for today. Take out the feathers from Burl's mattress, wash them and spread them out on the attic floor to dry."

"I didn't bring any old clothes with me."

"Never fear, dearie, I have an old dress that will protect that fussy dress of yours. Come up to the attic."

Susanna climbed the scuffed stairs behind Erna. Dust swirled lazily in the sunlight coming through the window as she stepped into the attic.

"Burl hauled up the mattress and tubs for me earlier. He and Tom are helping Herb Wilson for the day. I wanted you all to myself. Here's your dress and here's a scarf for all that hair of yours."

Erna held out a smudgy beige dress and a skimpy brown scarf.

"Come on, get it on. I want this done before you go home."

Susanna took the clothes and pulled the dress over her head. It covered her like a shapeless, musty-smelling shroud. The scarf was so small that by the time she managed to tie its ends, her hair was squished flat on the top of her head.

"Not quite the beauty anymore, are you dearie?" said Erna with a smirk. "I think we're off to a good start. Now, get to work. I'll check on you in an hour."

Susanna felt humiliated. How did Erna know she looked

awful with no height in her front hair? Surely the scarf made her look all cheeks and mouth. Her favorite light blue dress had given her courage but it was now covered with this sack.

When she cut the threads on the tick, she almost choked on the stink from the feathers and then she squealed as a clump of bed bugs fell out. But she steadied herself with the heartfire breath and tried valiantly to hum from her heart. By the time the hour was up, Susanna had all the feathers removed from the tick and she was stirring them into the tepid water in the first tub.

Erna stomped into the attic. "I don't want you singing in this house," she said.

"Aunt Prudence allows me to hum. It helps me get things done and I think these feathers need all the help they can get. Don't you have enough chickens and geese? I'm sure Aunt Prudence would give you our extra feathers if you're short of them."

"How kind of you, dearie, to dole out feathers to your poor neighbor. You Mansfield women always act like you're lady bountiful. But I've got you all under my thumb and that's where you're going to stay."

"I don't think we'll fit under your thumb."

"Don't you be uppity with me, Sue dearie, or I'll start broadcasting your family's dark secret."

"If you do that, then there won't be any need for me to marry Burl."

Erna grabbed her by the shoulders. "You little…!" She let go of her as she noticed the frightened look in Susanna's eyes. "That's the face I want to see. Now finish this job or you'll find that lunch has come and gone without you." Erna smiled her gloating smile and left the room.

This is not going well, thought Susanna, as she moved over to the window. Aunt Prudence may have been strict but she never laid a hand on me. I've never been frightened of anyone before. I'm floundering in more than dirty water.

She could see Gideon across the meadow. In a minute she could be down the stairs and out the front door but then Erna would broadcast the secret.

Susanna knelt down on the floor and put her forehead on the cool windowpane. How can that woman possibly have a shiny self? I can't fight her. She'd out-mean me every time. So what could bring out that nicer self? There is only one thing I can think of to do and that's to get into my heart and stay there until I find a solution. Here I go. I'm going to place all my attention on my heart and hold on with all my might.

Susanna returned to the tubs. She began humming quietly, using every scrap of concentration to keep her voice coming from her heart. Her hum went into the soggy feathers as she used a large strainer to lift them from the soapy tub into the second tub of clear water. Then the hum flowed into the cleaner feathers as she scooped them up and let them drain.

This is fun, she thought, it really is. These feathers are starting to look respectable again. I can't believe it. I'm actually enjoying this.

She hummed happily as she dropped the wet feathers on an old sheet. Rolling them up safely inside she used all her strength to wring out the sheet over the tub. Then she unrolled it and looked at the feathers.

These feathers deserve a clean floor, she thought. So she took off the scarf and dress and dusted the attic floor with them. Then she spread out the damp feathers. Would they be dry be the end of the day? She refused to worry.

I can't hum around Erna, she thought, but I can think a hum. She smiled at this as she felt a sweet tingle in her heart.

She skipped down the attic steps. "Mrs. Ringwurst, the feathers are drying."

"In here!" called Erna from the parlor. She sat in an old rocker, strategically placed in front of the window, where she could watch the main road that circled the meadow.

"You know, I actually enjoyed myself," said Susanna. "And

I've worked up an appetite. Can I help you get lunch?"

Erna scowled but Susanna just smiled back.

"See what you can find in the pantry and lay it out on the table. Call me when it's ready."

Susanna pulled up the crooked green shade on the pantry window, which left a spider dangling on his broken web. Chipped pieces of Erna's china, jars and bottles cluttered the shelves.

When she reached for a jar of preserves she thought of Aunt Violet's jellies. Maybe she could put some music in Erna's preserves. Susanna quietly closed the pantry door. Remembering Erna's shiny self, she started humming. She concentrated on the picture and the melody became pleasing to her ear. Then she tried to imagine the tune and the picture going into the preserves. A delightful tickle sprouted in her heart and a ribbon of colors spiraled from her chest and flowed into the jar. She almost dropped the jar. I've created magic, she thought. It works!

I need some bread for the jam, Susanna thought, as she opened the bread box. There's a loaf of Erna's famous bread—famous, because she always comes in second behind Gerda's mother at the spring fair. Here's some cheese to go with it. I hope she has some decent tea.

Susanna opened the pantry door and stepped into the kitchen. Ten minutes later she had the table set and the tea steeping.

"Lunch is ready, Mrs. Ringwurst."

Erna stopped as soon as she saw the table. A single daffodil leaned out of the empty preserve jar beside Erna's place.

"I don't see why you had to go mussing and fussing with that flower. I like a plain table." She sat down at the head of the table and Susanna sat at the other end.

"I see you know how to cut thin slices of bread," said Erna, as she reached for a piece and then dabbed it with preserves. "You certainly can't cut them thin from Leah Thompson's loaves. They're too cake-like in texture. Yet she wins that spring fair contest every time. My loaves look better, they slice better and they keep longer. There's no justice. Goodness, but these preserves are tasty today."

Susanna smiled to herself. What will happen now, she wondered, as she watched Erna reach for another slice of bread and slather it with preserves?

"Maybe you'll have better luck this year," she said. "Aunt Maisy started peeling last year's apples, so we're getting lots of desserts. She likes to practice way ahead of time for the fall apple-peeling contest. I'm proud she's the fastest in Spring Gate. Last year it looked like she was cutting her peel too thin and it would drop off, but she knows some tricks to keep it in one long curl."

"She'll probably win again. You Mansfield's! Your apples win at the fall fair, and at the spring fair, folks are always falling over themselves to buy your seedlings and bedding plants. I think you go around at night and paint your flowers to make them so bright—too bright for my taste. Folks can never get those colors to stay after they take the plants home."

As Erna grabbed the last of the bread, Susanna felt hopeful. Erna was saying her usual kind of remarks, but her tone was different. Was it possible that she looked just a wee bit younger too?

"Well now, Sue, you take your time with the dishes. I don't know if those feathers will be dry before you have to leave. But don't worry. I'll get Burl to deal with it. He usually does it anyway. Mind you, he gets embarrassed if I tell anyone. Why don't you join me at the window when you're finished? I get a splendid view of all the comings and goings of the village. It can occupy me for hours. That's why bread making suits me so well. There's lots of waiting."

By the time the afternoon had worn down, Susanna was feeling more hopeful. Erna was almost likeable. She chatted away about every person that came into view. There wasn't much that she did not know about why they were out and about. Then she gave a detailed history of their lives. Susanna could have done without the history. She preferred not to know some of the things that Erna knew.

But surely this was a good sign, she thought. Erna was treating her like a friend and friends were not mean to each other. Maybe, just maybe, she'd change her mind about wanting her to marry Burl.

Late in the afternoon, Erna leaned forward in her chair. "There's your hired man, Sue. I guess it's time for you to leave. My goodness, but I enjoyed your company. Who would have thought?"

She walked Susanna to the front door and watched while she wrapped Aunt Violet's shawl around her shoulders.

"That's right," said Erna, "it's still shawl weather. I'd like to see you again. You're good company. Come on over the day after tomorrow. I can get rid of the men for half a day. Keep me company while I make my bread. Make sure you're in time to prepare lunch for me."

Susanna had to ask: "Are you still thinking about me and Burl?"

Erna looked blank for a moment. "Well, I'll be," she said. "I'd plum forgot about that."

Susanna heaved a sigh of relief.

"Yes," said Erna. "I want you more than ever now. You're good to have around. I can see why Prudence changed her mind about the marriage. She wants you for herself. She can't have you. You're mine. Now, off you go. No holding hands with that fellow. You're spoken for."

As Erna was speaking, Susanna could see her tattered coat thinning in places and a light starting to twinkle through. Perhaps it was her shiny self trying to burst the seams of the old coat. But as Erna went on talking, she seemed to clutch that coat closer, as if a wind was blowing and she needed a good grip.

Susanna stumbled down the front steps and made her way over to Gideon.

"Tell me all about it," he said, as they slowly took the path past the general store and into the Mansfield's woods.

Susanna let out a huge sigh. "My plan worked too well. I performed magic, you know, real magic. A melody, like a colored ribbon, came out of my heart and flew into Erna's preserves. She did change, she became nicer, but now she thinks I'm good to have around. I have this crazy vision of being married to Burl and always humming into the food so Erna wouldn't be mean."

"You know your Melody Tales, don't you?"

"Yes."

"Remember the history of the people when they left the secret valley. It took them a long time to change from their shiny selves into those ordinary beings. So you can't expect things to change back in one afternoon over preserves."

"I don't have centuries to change Erna. I have a month."

Gideon stopped just before the path branched off to the Mansfield's. He placed both his hands on her shoulders.

"My favorite wood to carve is hardwood. I didn't like it at first when I was a boy and my father made me start my first task on a piece of oak. But I've learned that even though it's tougher to work with, the finished cupboard has lines and curves that you couldn't get in a softer wood and they last."

She looked into his eyes and smiled. "My father said that too. I guess you could say that I'm carving with my humming. I'll keep humming away and hopefully before my birthday she'll fall into more agreeable lines. Thank you. You know, it's strange that you and Aunt Violet happened to move here just before this trouble with Erna started."

"Aunt Violet thought it was time you remembered your musical connections."

"Nice, very nice—and very evasive."

That night Susanna sat up in bed. Her body was tired but her mind kept revolving the day's events.

After being in Erna's house, her room seemed precious to her. She had painted the walls herself, secretly adding a cup of pink dye to the whitewash. Her pink and blue quilt was extra puffy with wool. The curtains were her crowning achievement. She had found the gossamer fabric in her mother's trunk. Aunt Maisy helped her fashion them into curtains and Aunt Prudence showed her how to make the ruffles even protesting the whole time about how frivolous they were.

They blew gently in the evening's breeze. Just like the curtains in her music room, she thought. I'm sure that window is always open. Not like this window where Aunt Prudence checks it each night to make sure it's closed. Surely I don't have to be at Aunt Violet's to get into that room. The entrance to it is supposed to be in my heart.

She threw back the covers and sat on the side of her bed facing the window. Closing her eyes she tried to visualize the room, its pink chair and the flower with the diamond in its center.

The brambles! She was on the inner pathway to her music room and they had sprung up in front of her, droning, keening, sobbing and entreating her to listen to their tales of woe.

I shouldn't listen, she thought. But one off key tune inched its tendril towards her and then stopped at her feet. It lay there, quivering, but not moving closer.

Why do I feel so tired, she wondered? Maybe I should sit down for a few moments to rest.

The bramble's tendril still did not move. It only droned, louder and louder.

I don't know why I'm bothering with this quest anyway, she thought. I'll probably die young like my parents. What's the point of getting all excited about life when I'm not going to be around for long. Who cares about finding the singer? She probably isn't real anyway. Why am I going to all this bother?

I should just let my aunts get themselves out of trouble. I don't have to marry anyone I don't want to. I could care less if I was shunned. Gosh, I feel so weary.

And then the tendril curled and twirled around her ankles.

I'll move in a moment, she thought.

The whole bramble hedge moved closer and then she heard the other tune—the shrill one that made her heart close and her breath come swiftly. She was going to see something she had never wanted to see. She was not sure what it was but she knew it would terrify her.

The plant tightened its grip on her ankles. And then she tried to move. But she couldn't and the bramble came closer and its tune opened up the beginning of a memory and Susanna thought she would grow mad with the fear. Help me, she cried.

Deep within her heart a tiny door opened and a thought came through—quiet, calm and simply put. As she looked in its direction she began to be within the protection of its quiet. Within its stillness she heard its words.

"Within the heart of everything, even the music that drones, dwells a thread of love. Look to the love and the droning will disappear."

"The fear is too big," she said.

"It is a mirage," said the thought. "Take your attention off it and it will lose its power. Put your attention on the thread of love and sing."

Susanna began to hum, resting her voice on the thought's calmness. Her melody was simple, like a lullaby.

The tendril loosened on her ankles. The brambles receded.

After a few moments they disappeared. The picture of her music room became clear, as if it suddenly shifted into focus. In the next instant, she found herself inside the room, sitting in her chair.

The flower petals unfolded from the diamond and Susanna searched its many facets, looking for one that would be the doorway to lead her to the problem's solution.

One facet called out to her and as she looked into its mirror-like surface it grew larger and larger. Soon she could step through its doorway. The pillared house stood there and the music with its colored ribbons of sound floated before her.

The main floor hallway appeared to be the same. She moved swiftly up the stairs to the fourth floor. At the end of the hall, just before the stairs to the next floor, a door stood open. Stale air hung in the opening as if it hadn't the strength to go further. Susanna moved cautiously through it and stood on a balcony overlooking Spring Gate.

The valley spread out before her. It was daytime and everything seemed entwined with dusty brambles. At each beat of a droning rhythm brown dust rose in the air and then settled on the valley and its people.

I don't want to breathe it in or listen to it, she thought, as she stepped back into the hallway and shut the balcony door. I've had enough of that.

She climbed to the fifth floor and walked down the length of the hall. Before the next circular stairway another door stood open. This time the air was fresh and the music flowed from the opening, so she went through to stand on its balcony.

The music wafted round her face. As she breathed it in, the melody began to throb in every part of her. When her heart overflowed she started to hum. A stream of colored light rippled from her. Spring Gate was still spread out before her, but Susanna's rolling melody dissolved the brambles and the world turned bright and crispy clear. Every part of the valley now rang with its own music, perfectly in-tune.

Her melody met the trees' songs and sang with them. The trees lifted their branches and the mingled threads of color and sound flowed from leaf to twig, to branch, to trunk, and to root. As the song touched the earth, it blended with the melodies of the grass and flowers. The earth's song coursed to the banks of Sweetwater Creek and the water's bubbling tune rose up to absorb it.

The ribbon of her song then rolled back to her, bringing all the music it had harmonized with. She knew in that moment, when the wave of music washed gently against her, that she heard a love song—threads of individual melodies blending perfectly together.

Then she was back in her bedroom, sitting on the side of the bed and still tingling with the music. The moonlight shone through her window and there on the sill was the tiniest, most exquisite creature she had ever seen. A fairy!

Chapter
Nine

SUSANNA GETS THE PICTURE

Fidelity, clasped her hands in delight. "At last!" "Oh, you can see me!"

Susanna stared and then said: "You're wearing a dress just like my favorite blue one."

"Of course."

"Where do you come from?" asked Susanna.

"From the valley within the Melody Mountains."

"The Secret Valley?" asked Susanna, leaning closer to look at Fidelity.

"We call it Songspun."

"I knew the valley was real! I'm going there to look for a beautiful woman with the most wonderful voice. Perhaps you know her."

"Many beautiful women live there and they're all good singers."

"Do you have a name?"

"Fidelity and I'm yours, I'm your very own fairy."

"What do you mean?"

"I've been assigned to you. That's a great honor for someone like me who just graduated."

"Graduated?" asked Susanna as she wiggled her way to the top of the bed and sat back against her pillows. She patted the quilt beside her after putting her legs under the covers.

"Yes, from the fairy picture school," said Fidelity flying to Susanna's side and daintily arranging her blue dress as she sat down. "Usually after graduation we have to apprentice at our specialty for two years but my teacher thought I could do the job. She tested me; of course, to make sure I was capable. I had to hold the picture of a music ribbon in my mind for five whole minutes. It's hard work but, you see, I love those ribbons. That's what I'm specializing in."

"I read about fairies and Amy and I liked to pretend they were real but you're beyond anything I ever imagined. You're very pretty and your voice sounds like a sweet bell. Did you just arrive here?"

"No, I've been here almost a month."

"I'm sorry I didn't see you before."

"That's quite all right."

"What do you mean you're going to specialize?"

"At school we had to picture whatever our teacher showed us. We learned to put every ounce of our attention on the picture inside our mind and when we could do that without a wobble, we learned to create it outside of us. 'First you see it inside and then you create it outside.' That's the saying we learned. For my beginning lesson my teacher sent the picture of one blade of grass into my mind. After that I learned how to make it grow. Then I got a whole field to look after and later on I put in flowers. Just before graduation we were allowed to choose what we really like to picture."

"You're interested in ribbons?" asked Susanna, as she remembered the ribbons of color she had put into Erna's preserves.

"I love all the things that are like rainbows, like the ribbons of colored melody that come from you when you sleep." Fidelity stood up and flew to the top of the pillow. She stuck her little face close to Susanna's ear. "Every night since I've been here I curl up on the pillow and listen to the song that comes from you. It gives me wonderful dreams."

Susanna looked at the little form beside her head. She smiled and Fidelity smiled back at her.

"I guess you're the same as people," she said, moving further under the covers. "We have favorite things we like to do. I like to make up tunes. Aunt Maisy loves to cook. Aunt

Prudence loves to keep our home in perfect order. Erna is keen about making bread. Having something you like doing makes life interesting. Wait a minute, wait a minute!"

She sat back up again.

"What's the matter?" asked Fidelity, fluttering in front of her.

"I'm getting a wonderful idea," said Susanna. "Oh, it's a great idea! I know how to get Erna to change her mind about me and Burl. And you can help."

"Oh goody!" said Fidelity doing a graceful spin in the air.

"I'll compose a song and then I'll teach it to you."

"I love to learn songs."

"Too bad you didn't have some friends. I have a feeling a whole choir would be useful."

"Come over to the window," said Fidelity as she flew to the sill. "Look outside."

Susanna knelt at her window and looked out on the moonlit yard. Colored lights shone in the trees, around the flowers and in the grass. Within the lights were tiny fairies. The world outside was full of them. Susanna's eyes filled with tears.

"They're so lovely. Have they always been here?" she asked.

"Yes. There are some excellent singers among them. Gustafus has trained them."

"Gustafus?"

"Gideon's gnome helper."

"I have been blind, haven't I?" said Susanna.

"That's perfectly all right. You've hummed and that has made a big difference to my friends."

"Time to go to sleep, Fidelity. We have a big day ahead of us tomorrow. I can't wait to tell Aunt Prudence and Aunt Maisy my idea. I won't tell them about you or the other fairies, though. I don't think they're ready for that."

Susanna got back into bed and snuggled under the covers. She smiled as Fidelity settled on the pillow.

"Goodnight Fidelity." "Goodnight Susanna."

The morning sun filtered through the vines outside the kitchen window as Susanna and her aunts finished breakfast.

"So," said Aunt Prudence, dabbing her mouth carefully with her serviette, "Your whole future depends on persuading Erna to sing a song?"

"I'm sure it will work," said Susanna, taking the dishes to the dish pan. "I need to change her into her nicer self and a good song should do it, if I can get her to sing it, that is. Since she desperately wants her bread to win first prize at the fair, she might try this. Nothing has worked for her so far."

"It's not a solution in my opinion. Erna requires something more powerful, like a thunderbolt, to make her change her mind."

"I know what you mean, but I feel strongly about this."

"I'd look for thunder and lightning if I were you," said Aunt Prudence, gathering up the table cloth and taking it to the back door to shake out the crumbs.

Later that day Gideon met Susanna at her favorite spot. She had just come from Aunt Violet's. Susanna sat on her rock humming and then singing some words to her melody.

"I'm glad you're here," she said. "Aunt Violet thought the song idea was good but she said you could give me some advice on how to keep firing up the magic. What does she mean?"

Gideon leaned back on his elbows. "I guess she wants me to tell you that you have to believe that you will succeed. That's what I was taught. No matter what the appearances might be, no matter how Erna acts, you must keep on believing that it's all going to work out. Believing is like blowing on hot coals and doubt is like throwing dirt on the fire."

Susanna looked to where Gustafus was leaning against a tree chatting with Fidelity. "Will you allow Gustafus to teach the fairies the song I'm composing? Fidelity tells me that he's been conducting them already."

"Good idea. The more music, the bigger the magic. Gustafus, did you hear that? When Susanna has her song ready, you can get the fairies together to practice."

Gustafus moved away from the tree and gave a short bow to Susanna. "I'm yours to command."

"Thank you. I'm sorry it's taken me so long to notice you. I hope I didn't hurt your feelings."

"I accept your apology. Sometimes it's not a bad thing to be invisible to people. But I won't allow the fairies to go inside Erna's house. Its droning sound would make them sing out-of-tune."

"I'll open the kitchen window and they could gather just outside."

"That would be all right," he said, hitching up his pants. "Fairies aren't as tough as we gnomes."

The next morning Aunt Prudence and Aunt Maisy heard Susanna's song drift through the house. Later they heard her talking to herself as she did her chores.

"I'm rehearsing what I can say to Erna," she said in answer to Aunt's Prudence's comment that people would think she was addled if they ever heard her.

They watched her walk down the path with Gideon and then shook their heads in unison.

"It's the first song I've composed with words," said Susanna, walking beside Gideon. "I'm so nervous. What if this doesn't work? No, don't answer that. It will work."

They were almost at Erna's house when Gideon stopped. "I'll be here to walk you home. I'll leave you now so Erna won't get in a snit. I want her in a reasonable mood to start with."

She turned towards Erna's front door. Squaring her shoulders, she knocked.

"Come on in," called Erna from her favorite chair in the parlor.

Susanna walked into the house and hung her shawl on the hook beside the front door. She took a jar of amber jelly from her skirt pocket.

"I brought you some of my Aunt Violet's jelly for our lunch," she said in the parlor doorway. "I'll start fixing it right away."

"Harrumph," said Erna, as she faced the window again.

She's back to her sour ways, thought Susanna, as she filled the kettle with fresh water and put it over the fire. Erna's bread dough was rising nicely in its bowl on the stove's warming shelf. When she finished cutting slices from some day old bread and putting her aunt's jelly into a small bowl, she opened the kitchen window. Gustafus and the fairies were under the apple trees at the edge of the yard.

Erna ambled into the kitchen and took her place at the head of the table.

"My preserves are just as good as your aunt's jelly," she said. "I fail to see why everyone raves about it. Jelly is jelly."

"Aunt Violet has a special ingredient."

"And what might that be?" asked Erna.

"It's a secret. I'm the only one in the village who knows what it is."

"I'm not the least bit curious."

Susanna smiled and helped herself to the jelly. She spread a modest amount on her bread and then she set it right in front of Erna's plate.

Erna's nostrils twitched and she shook her head slightly. Another bit of twitching. With a begrudging sigh she spooned some jelly onto her bread.

"Well, I'll see what all the fuss is about."

After the first bite she ate steadily away.

"Not bad, not bad. Crabapple isn't it? And something else? I can't place it. It's not honey or sugar or lemon. It must be an unusual apple. Did you only bring one jar?"

After Erna had three more slices of bread, she heaved herself to her feet.

"Put the dishes in the pan, Sue. It's time to watch me punch down my bread and knead it again."

Erna set the bowl of bread dough on the table after Susanna cleared the dishes away. Then she opened her flour bin and scooped out some flour. When she had the center of the table nicely dusted with it she lifted the damp cloth from the bowl. "Perfect," she said with a satisfied sigh. "Do you know what my secret ingredient is? I'll tell you. It's milk. Yes, that's right. That's what makes my bread keep longer and makes it tender yet firm with that nice creamy color."

"Then why does Gerda's mom always win first prize at the fair," asked Susanna with innocent eyes.

"Darned if I know," she said, punching her fist into the dough, with more vigor than necessary. She scooped it out, plopped it on the table and began to knead it ruthlessly. "We buy the same flour, the same sugar, the same yeast. I knead mine exactly the right amount of time. Whenever I make bread I think of her and my thoughts go on a high boil. What in this ordinary world can she be doing that makes those dimwitted judges choose her bread over mine? I'd give anything to know."

Susanna's eyes lit up. "I know a secret ingredient that would make your bread win first prize."

Erna stopped kneading. "I don't believe you."

"I figured you wouldn't," she said, taking off her apron. This was the key moment. She trembled but forced herself to look confident.

"Where are you going?" demanded Erna.

"I may as well leave. You obviously don't think a young person like me would know such things, even though my aunt's jellies have become so popular in the village that most ladies are talking about buying them this fall rather than putting up their own. She allows me to help her so I've found out what the ingredient is and it's something you could easily use in bread making. But, since you're not interested, I'll be going."

"Not so fast," said Erna. "Let me think, let me think." She looked down at her bread and automatically began to knead it.

"All it needs is one special ingredient to win first prize," said Susanna, slowly hanging up her apron.

I give in" said Erna clasping her doughy hands together. "If I could win, I'd burst my buttons. No one would care if my house had dust or grime because I'd be the best bread maker in the valley. It's been my dream since my aunt first taught me. That's the only domestic thing I learned. My mother was too sick to teach me about cooking and cleaning. All right. I'll keep kneading and you tell me what it is. I'll try it out in my next batch."

"You could put it in now. The secret ingredient comes from your heart, it goes into your hands and then it goes into the bread. It's simple. What you think and what you feel goes into your bread. If you have sour thoughts then you'll have sour bread. I can teach you a song that will make your bread so good tasting that Gerda's mom can't possibly win."

"You want me to sing to my bread!"

"I know it sounds silly but it works. Why do you think our apples are the best tasting in the valley? I sing to them and the trees love it."

"It's crazy! I don't believe it. What if someone heard me?" asked Erna, looking towards the window.

"Sing quietly. If someone is around, you can sing just in your mind. Of course, if you don't believe me then I probably should leave."

"No! Teach me the song. I'll look stupid but I have to win. Come on, what are the words. I can sing. I liked to sing those school songs, you know—'Ordinary Virtues' and 'Ordinary Work.'"

"All right," said Susanna. "But remember, you have to do it exactly as I say or it won't work."

"Teach me the silly song!"

"I will. I'll sing it a few times, slowly, and you follow along. Don't let any nasty thoughts come into your mind. Well, they might come in by accident, of course, but don't let them make themselves at home. Here we go," she said, and stepping close to the open window she began to sing.

Making bread happy is my ploy.
Let the yeast bubble up with joy.
Knead the dough soft yet strong,
Filling it all with this song.
Roll it, turn it, flour it some.
It will be good to the last crumb.
From my heart, then to my hand,
Love flows into each bread pan.
Sing a song of sweet tasting bread.
Love's the magic that all are fed.
Let it rise and rise and rise,
To the very highest prize.

The fairies hovered outside the window and followed Gustafus' conducting. Their little voices sang an octave higher than Susanna's, and Erna's voice, at first hesitant and self conscious, followed along in her deep alto. Then she began to get into the rhythm and kneaded the bread in time to it.

No one would recognize her, thought Susanna, as she watched her swaying happily rolling and turning the dough. Erna sang as she cut the dough into four equal parts and then formed them into loaves. She gently fitted them into the pans and covered them with the damp cloth as if she were tucking children in for their naps.

"I'm getting the hang of it, aren't I," said Erna. "This will win me first prize?"

"Only if you keep out sour thoughts. Remember they don't taste good. Just picture people eating your bread and feeling happy. Promise me you'll sing the song and put your heart into it?"

"It's crazy, it's downright crazy, but I'll do it," said Erna as she slapped a floury hand on Susanna's shoulder.

"I want to tell you something, Susanna," said Aunt Prudence, as she brought the tea to the supper table that night.

"Maisy and I feel that the best way to stop Erna from ruining your life is to…sell our…home and move. We'll find a place where nobody knows us. We should have enough gold to give us a new start."

Susanna stood up and then sat down. "But…but…Aunt Prudence, you don't need to do that! Erna has agreed to sing my song."

Aunt Maisy patted her hand. "We don't want to hurt your feelings dear, but a song is not the solution. This situation needs drastic measures and we're prepared to give up our life here."

"But you can't!" cried Susanna. "Mansfield's have lived in this spot for centuries. Why whenever I see that crumbling stone railing with its broken pillar in the corner of the orchard, I realize how old this place is. Even the root cellar was once the cellar of the very first house. You can't do this! Have some faith in me."

"No Susanna, we can't chance it. I've already written to Amy's parents in Harlowville." Aunt Prudence pulled a letter from her apron pocket. "I just heard back from them and they have found someone who wants to buy this place. I didn't think there would be any trouble selling because Spring Gate will look mighty good to those folks suffering crop failures out on the plains."

Susanna got up and went over to Aunt Prudence and put her arms around her. "Don't sell. Give me some time."

Aunt Prudence sniffed and dabbed at her eyes with her napkin. "We have three weeks until the fair and your coming-of-age birthday is three days after that. By then there'll be no excuse to put off the marriage for I'm sure Erna will want to marry you to Burl right after your birthday." She patted Susanna's arms. "We won't discuss it anymore, please. Our minds are made up and that's that. Now, sit down and finish your tea before it gets cold. Let's discuss what needs to be done for the fair. Perhaps Gideon could repair our old booth. The front counter is wobbly."

Chapter
Ten

THE PRIZE

The best events of the year were the fairs but then they were the only events of each ordinary year. People were hard pressed not to feel some happiness and there was music aplenty with the traveling singers. The singers used their music to dissolve the shades of gloom that hung over a village. Ribbons of their songs curled around the fair booths.

Fairies were able to fly all over the village green without getting their wings coated with the gloom. They played hopscotch on a quilt in one booth, leaping from one bland colored diamond pattern to another. At the broom booth they pushed the straws apart and glided hand in hand between the shafts. Inside the Thompson's booth they pulled the tassels on the tea cozies as if they were bells.

Mrs. Thompson gave a delicate snort as the motion caught her eye. She had told Gerda more than once they were too fancy. A simple knot would not have wasted so much yarn. Gerda had paid no attention to her mother's scolding because Susanna, whose booth was beside theirs, had told her yesterday that she hoped to have some good news for her regarding Burl.

The fairies lingered at Susanna's booth chatting to Fidelity and Gustafus. The usual Mansfield products were for sale—apple tree seedlings—which were famous beyond Spring Gate, apple pies made from dried apples, and plants that Susanna and Aunt Prudence had nurtured under glass frames—sensible vegetable seedlings by Aunt Prudence and rose bushes hummed into small blossoms by Susanna.

For three days the wagons and tents from people living beyond the valley had filled the village green beside the booths. Now the fair was winding down and everyone was looking forward to the afternoons judging.

"I'm sorry you couldn't get all the finely milled flour you wanted," said Susanna, as she stood behind the front counter of their booth watching the judging tables being set up.

Aunt Maisy sat in her chair counting the coins from her apron pocket. "It certainly is a disappointment. I depend on that for my cakes. Jake said the drought on the plains is making it scarce and expensive. He's almost out of the past summer's wheat and usually he has more than enough supply until the next fall harvest. Well, I'll have enough for your birthday."

Susanna watched as the judges brought the top two entries in each category to the tables. "If only we didn't have to wait for the bread making results. Why do they put it last each year?"

"Probably they don't want Erna sulking during the rest of the judging. She casts a dark cloud on things. Although, you know, it's the funniest thing—I actually heard her compliment her husband yesterday. She said he'd done a good job on grafting two types of apple trees. I haven't heard her say anything nice to him for years."

"Other people have mentioned how she's getting nicer."

"Yes dear, but has she said anything to you about not marrying Burl?"

"No, but I'm hoping when she wins the contest she'll have a change of heart."

By mid afternoon all the judging was done, except for the bread. Henry, from the general store, and Dean Foremost, the Mayor, stood before the table.

Two identical loaves sat there—same golden crust, same height, same thickness, and same freshly baked smell. But they sang a different song and only Susanna, Gideon and the fairies could hear and see the music.

Erna's loaf was on the right and Susanna was pleased that

Erna had followed her instructions and put her heart into the song. Wispy ribbons of pink, blue and white curled into the air above the loaf and the song rang from the colors.

Mrs. Thompson's loaf sat on the left. Its music of bland ribbons curled up one moment and then plopped down the next. The song came out in spurts.

Oh no! Oh no!
Is my yeast supply too low?
Oh dear! Oh dear!
Will it rise enough this year?
Oh my! Oh my!
Now the mix looks much too dry.
Oh well! Oh well!
Hope I win, but who can tell?

The judges cut a small slice from the loaves and chewed thoughtfully. Then they nodded to each other and Henry pinned the first place ribbon on Erna's. Moving to Mrs. Thompson's he stuck in the second place ribbon.

The crowd stood in shocked silence until Susanna started clapping and then several people joined in. Henry held up his hand for silence.

"This year we have a new winner of the bread making contest—Erna Ringwurst and second place to Louisa Thompson. As head of the spring fair committee I now declare this year's a wonderful success and I also declare it over. Thank you all for your efforts."

People started moving away from the judging tables. Whispered comments floated in the air: "Can you believe it! Erna!" "There'll be no living with her now!" A few ladies stopped to congratulate her. Soon only she and Susanna remained gazing at the loaves and their ribbons. They turned and looked at each other. Erna threw her arms around her and gave her a bear hug.

"It worked! It worked! You dear little thing. I know you made this possible. Where's Tom? Wait till I tell him. Oh my goodness! I'm about to burst my seams I'm so happy. Well, I'll see you later, Sue. I feel so good; I'm going to call you Susanna from now on. Your aunts are heading this way. I'll wait and let them congratulate me."

Erna beamed on Aunt Prudence and Aunt Maisy as they walked up to her.

"Congratulations, Erna," said Prudence, shaking her hand.

"My congratulations too," said Maisy, giving her fingers for Erna to shake.

"Isn't it wonderful!" gushed Erna. "Just between us four, I owe it to Susanna here." She put an arm around her. "I intend to keep this girl by me all the time. I used to think it would be good to have a daughter and that's how I'm starting to think of her. Oh, oh, here comes your hired man. Remember what I said about holding hands, Susanna. Well, I've got to find Tom."

She gave Susanna a last squeeze and then scurried away.

Gideon joined the ladies and arched an eyebrow at Susanna.

"No," she said. "It hasn't worked."

"I told you it would take a lot more than a song to change Erna," said Aunt Prudence. "Gideon, you will stay with us until we move, won't you? We could surely use your help."

"I'll be here," he said. "But you won't have to move."

"You know we're expecting the papers for the sale any day now. Once Maisy and I have signed, that's it. According to the buyer's request, we'll have only a week to be out."

"There's still time," said Gideon.

"There's time for dreaming, maybe," said Aunt Prudence, turning away.

Gideon and Susanna stayed beside each other as the aunts walked back to the booth. He took her hand and looked into her eyes. "There *is* still time. Don't give up. Don't even act like you've given up."

"But..."

"No buts. It's like climbing a mountain. If you look down you might lose your nerve. Keep looking at the peak."

On the morning of Susanna's birthday, she ran down the stairs, determinedly ignoring the boxes of linen, china and rugs stacked in the hallway. This was the final day for the song to work. Every waking hour of the past weeks felt like it had been painstakingly carved through time. She had never noticed her thoughts so much before, but every time she tried to concentrate on the pictures of her song's victory, doubts and fears would pop up and try to distract her.

Gideon had likened it to mountain climbing, but never having climbed one she thought instead of the wire and board fence surrounding the vegetable garden that she and Amy had often balanced across when they were younger. Sometimes, walking the top board, they had tried to make the other giggle by saying silly things. They wanted to see who would be the first to lose their balance and fall off.

But this wasn't a game with only a short fall to the soft earth. Her whole future and the happiness of her aunts depended on her not paying attention to the doubts and fears. It was the hardest work she'd ever done. She felt she was walking that board fence and at every step, tentacles of droning thoughts tried to grab her. She was sure she had wrinkles in her forehead trying to keep her attention on that vision of her home with happiness beaming from it like sunshine.

"Good morning!" she called out as she walked into the kitchen.

"Happy Birthday, dear," said Aunt Prudence as she stirred the porridge. "I'll be glad to help you pack up your bedroom after your birthday dinner is over."

"No thank you," she said, getting the bowls and spoons from the pantry and putting them on the table. "Remember, I'm not planning on having to move."

"Susanna, you're carrying this too far. There's so much to do. You haven't even begun to pack the upstairs sitting room."

"Let's just concentrate on my birthday right now. Where

has Aunt Maisy hidden my cake? I've checked the pantry and it's not there. It smelled like it was baking forever yesterday, so it must be huge."

Aunt Prudence smiled and shook her head. "All right. Put out some butter plates too. Erna insisted on giving me some of her bread yesterday. As if we don't have our own! Let's try some of your Aunt Violet's pear jelly. I could use some pep for all we have to do."

Aunt Maisy came slowly into the kitchen. She held a large envelope in her hands. "These are the papers for the sale. Henry just dropped them off. He said they came in late yesterday on the grocery wagon." She gingerly put the envelope on the table beside Prudence's plate. Everyone looked at it as if they wished it weren't there.

"Promise me you won't sign anything on my birthday?" pleaded Susanna. "Let's leave this day just for a family celebration, as if nothing is wrong in our worlds. Let's pretend, for today, that we'll always live here. Please. It can't hurt."

Maisy nodded her head slightly at Prudence.

"As you wish, dear," said Aunt Prudence. "We'll give you today as a present. Maisy, put that envelope in a pantry drawer where we won't have look at it."

The birthday dinner was held late afternoon on the front lawn. Aunt Violet had been invited, and Fidelity, at Susanna's request, had invited the fairies. Susanna brought out the box of her mother's ribbons and hung them from the cherry tree that shaded the dinner table.

"Why in the world are you doing that?" asked Aunt Prudence when she saw her tying the ribbons by one end so they fluttered in the breeze.

"I'd like a little color in my world," she answered, smiling up at the fairies, some who had begun to swing back and forth on the ribbons.

"Well, I do believe we're ready. And here comes Violet. "Good afternoon, Violet. Perfect day for a birthday, isn't it."

Aunt Violet smiled and kissed Susanna's cheek. "Prudence, you must let me help you. What can I do?"

"Nothing, Violet, it's all ready. Gideon is helping Maisy in the kitchen, so all we have to do is sit out here and enjoy the sunshine."

The dinner progressed through the corn mush soup, delicately flavored with nutmeg and cinnamon, and then through the acorn and bean casserole topped with mounds of baking powder dumplings. As the meal finished, Aunt Maisy nodded to Gideon. They stacked the dirty dishes on trays and disappeared inside the house.

Susanna couldn't keep the smile off her face. She loved birthdays.

"Close your eyes, Susanna," called Gideon from the doorway. "And don't open them until I say so."

She squeezed her eyes shut and listened to the swish, swish of Aunt Maisy's skirt getting closer, the firm step of Gideon and then the velvety plunk as the plate touched the tablecloth in front of her.

"Now you can open them."

It was an amazing cake. Squares and triangles formed the shape of her home. A roof of green icing topped it and green candy sticks outlined the windows. Fidelity hovered beside it and then she pulled on a string on the far side of the cake. The windows lit up, for an instant, as if there were lights inside each room and Susanna was reminded of the home of her dream. She gasped, but as she looked at her two aunts she could tell they had not seen the flash.

"You made this?" she asked Aunt Maisy.

"Gideon designed it. He brought me the special cake pans and then he put it together after it was all baked. I, of course, made the cake itself. The windows are sugar sticks, so we can eat them too."

"It's magnificent," said Susanna, as she gazed at Gideon and then looked away. She felt shy of holding his gaze. How could he have known of her vision? But she couldn't help it; she had to take another peek at him. He slowly winked at her.

"Cut the cake," he said, "and I'd like a good sized piece."

Susanna served the cake. Everyone waited until she took her first bite.

"Hmm," she said, "Aunt Maisy you have outdone yourself. This is scrumptious."

"Thank you, dear," she said, trying not to look too pleased.

Everyone ate steadily away while the fairies flew around the cake trying unsuccessfully to enter the doors and windows.

"This has been a wonderful dinner, an incredible dessert," said Aunt Violet, after placing her napkin on the table. "I'm sorry to have to rush away but I have a batch of jelly to finish. Susanna, why don't you walk me home?"

"I'll be glad to," she said. "It's a Mansfield tradition that you don't have to do the dishes on your birthday." She winked at Gideon.

"I get the hint," he said. "Maisy, Prudence, allow me to wash. You ladies can dry because you know where everything goes. I hope this earns me another piece of cake."

Aunt Violet put an arm around Susanna's shoulder as they walked down the path with the fairies trooping beside them. "Let's not talk, dear. Why don't you hum? Find a melody that fits what you want this day to bring you. Picture the notes going out like tiny balls of light, carrying your melody and splashing it gently over everything and everyone they touch."

Susanna thought for a while until she got a feeling in her heart. Those feelings always held the melody. She let her voice sink into her heart as she began to hum.

"Very nice," said Aunt Violet, when they reached the edge of her field. "I won't ask you in. I've too much to do. If I were you, I'd hum all the way home."

Susanna and Fidelity returned down the path. By now it was twilight and the fairies walked beside them carrying lanterns. Once they were in the woods the light was dim and she could hear, as she paused to take a breath, the drone of the brambles. What were they doing here, she wondered? They had only been on the trail to her inner music room before. Maybe I'm always on that trail, she thought, no matter where I am.

A brown fog enveloped Susanna and the fairy's lanterns grew dimmer and dimmer.

She stopped. The droning grew louder. She could make out the thoughts of doubt and fear that she had been trying so hard to ignore.

I feel so tired, she thought. Her shoulders drooped. I'll just rest for a while. It can't hurt to listen to those thoughts for a moment or two. When I've had a nap I'll feel better.

"Stop," said Fidelity. "Stop! We don't like that sound. Look at our dress."

Susanna opened her eyes. Fidelity sat on the ground. She was covered in brown dust.

"No!" cried Susanna. "Leave her alone!" She reached down and picked up Fidelity. With her other hand she lifted a corner of her tiny dress and tried to shake it free from the dust. A brown cloud rose in the air and Fidelity began coughing.

Susanna covered her mouth and took a deep breath, a heartfire breath, and let her hum ring out.

The dust disappeared and her hum grew louder. The brambles faded away. Fidelity's dress grew clean and blue. The fairies appeared again along the sides of the path. They began to echo Susanna's melody and where their lanterns shone on the path the earth sparkled like gems.

When they reached the path leading to the Mansfield home the fairies stopped and swung their lanterns back and forth. Colored balls of light shot ahead of Susanna and Fidelity—lighting the way to the back door.

They paused on the step as soon as they heard Erna's voice booming out from the parlor.

"Oh no," whispered Susanna, "Do you think you can keep humming that song? It could help me get through this."

Fidelity perched on Susanna's shoulder and hummed in her bell-like voice as they walked through the back porch, into the kitchen, through the hall and then into the parlor where Erna was still talking away.

"There she is," said Erna, as Susanna entered. "She's the one that's responsible for the whole thing."

Susanna looked at her aunts. Aunt Maisy smiled her company smile as she bent over her mending and Aunt Prudence sat in her usual erect posture, after putting her teacup in its saucer.

"That's right," continued Erna, "if she hadn't helped me win the contest I wouldn't have seen things the way I do now. I was just telling your aunts of my plans for you. Goodness gracious, girl, can't you sit down in your own house."

Susanna sat on the stool beside the fireplace and waited for Erna to continue. Fidelity's humming tickled her ear.

"Like I was saying, I want you to know how I intend to take care of Burl and you."

Erna paused as she reached for her teacup. "First of all, there's the wedding to be considered." She took a sip and then another before she set her cup down. "This is excellent tea, Maisy. Susanna will have to show me how to make such a good brew. Now, where was I? Burl! You'd make him a good wife, Susanna and you would sure get my house shining, but I need to look at a bigger picture than that. Every time I sing that song, I think of him and how he's always been a meek little chap. He needs some oomph to him, something like the tang in this tea. I think you'd swamp him—you've got far too much tang, if you'll excuse me for saying so. Now Gerda, she's got just a pinch of tang, and that would suit him better. So, the long and the short of it is, I don't want you to marry my son. The idea has been coming at me for days but on this walk over I finally made up my mind."

Susanna sat up straight and couldn't think of a thing to say. It had worked, but she couldn't believe it yet.

"Yippee!" said Fidelity in her ear.

"I must confess I was looking forward to your company and having you keep my house clean, but the important thing is doing what's best for Burl. Gerda is a good enough housekeeper. And…regarding your, uh, secret, Prudence, I never would have told, you know. I was bluffing. I've never blabbed anyone's secret, although I confess I have hinted at it."

Aunt Prudence nodded her head graciously. Aunt Maisy stopped mending and beamed at Erna.

"That's that then. I guess beating Louisa Thompson has gone to my head because I'm thinking of experimenting. Maisy, what do you think of bread with a dash of cinnamon, brown sugar and melted butter swirled into the top of the dough? Too fancy?"

"It sounds rather delightful, Erna," said Maisy, as she put the mending into her sewing basket. "Surely a wee bit on top wouldn't be frowned on."

"That's what I thought. I'd better get going. Tom and Burl will be waiting for their tea. Susanna, come over from time to time and visit. You'll do that, won't you?"

"Absolutely," said Susanna rising from the stool and walking Erna to the door. "I'll have to come and taste your new recipe."

Her aunts lagged behind them as Susanna opened the door for Erna. Turning to her, she said, softly: "Thank you Mrs. Ringwurst. I'm so grateful you're letting Burl marry Gerda. She really loves him."

Erna gave her cheek a small pat as she went out the door. "Now, take care that you don't hold hands with that hired man of yours, not in public at least. Perhaps one of these days you could teach me a song that would help me keep my house clean."

"It's a miracle," said Aunt Maisy, from behind Susanna, as they watched Erna walk away. "I'd say I'm meeting Erna for the first time tonight. I actually like her. Isn't it wonderful,

Prudence? We can sleep well for the first time in a long while."

"Yes, indeed. We owe you a big apology, Susanna. I think a certain envelope would look good on top of the fire, don't you Maisy? Susanna you go and get it and bring it into the parlor."

When Susanna brought in the envelope the aunts were sitting around the fireplace.

"You put it on the fire, dear," said Aunt Prudence.

The envelope sat untouched for a tiny moment on the logs. Then the edges caught and flame rippled across the top. Layers of legal papers curled and blackened. Soon there were only the thin charred remains.

"I'll wash the tea things," said Susanna as she gathered them up and took them to the kitchen.

"That little girl has saved us all," said Aunt Maisy, after she left.

"She's not a little girl anymore."

"No, no she's not, Prudence. She's old enough to get married. If she wants to, of course."

The aunts sat in comfortable silence, looking at the fire.

"What do you think of Gideon?" asked Maisy.

"Let's not be thinking of matchmaking. I've learned my lesson."

"Of course, dear. I'll not mention it again."

Chapter Eleven

THE QUEST

Susanna hummed as she washed the tea dishes. Aunt Prudence insisted that a good housekeeper dried the dishes the moment they were washed, but she was too excited, so she left them draining on a tea towel. She cut a piece of cake and put it on a plate. Putting on her shawl she slipped out the back door and headed towards the workshop.

Fidelity whisked ahead of her and knocked on the door with her little fist.

Gustafus opened the door.

"Good evening," said Fidelity, "Susanna has something very important to tell Gideon."

"Back here, Susanna," called Gideon, from the corner of the shop. He was sitting at his table rubbing oil into a board. When Susanna came up to him, he gestured for her to take the seat opposite him. She put the cake on the table and sat down.

"The song worked! Erna left a short while ago and she's changed her mind! She's going to let Burl marry Gerda and she's not going to do anything nasty. I'm free! Isn't it wonderful!"

He put down his oiling rag and set the board on the bench behind him. Then he wiped his hands on a clean cloth. "I saw Erna coming earlier and I had a feeling she was bringing good news."

Susanna leaned back in the chair. "Yes, indeed. We burned the envelope with the sale papers right after she left. That was a glorious sight. You know what's next, don't you?"

"I like to think so."

"My quest, of course."

Gustafus raised his eyebrows and looked at Fidelity. She shrugged her shoulders.

Gideon scraped his chair closer to the table and took Susanna's hand. "Before you talk about that, I'm hoping you'll listen to what I have to say. Susanna, I feel like I've known you a long time and in some way I have. When I first saw you I knew you were the one I wanted to be with for the rest of my life. Do you understand? I love you and want to marry you."

Susanna's mouth opened in a silent 'oh'. She could only stare.

Fidelity tugged on Gustafus' sleeve and they both went to the other end of the shop but listened as hard as they could.

Gideon smiled as he observed Susanna's expression. "What do you feel for me?"

She closed her mouth, swallowed and tried to withdraw her hand. "I've always liked you. You're my friend."

"Like Amy?"

This time Susanna succeeded in tugging her hand free. She thought for a moment.

"No, not like Amy. I don't have anyone to compare you to. At school, the boys would tease and chat with the other girls, but not with me. I certainly don't think of you like I did my father. So, you're in your own special category, but friend seems like the best word. I honestly never thought of being married to you."

"Consider it now."

Susanna wished she could run away to think by herself. His presence was too alive and was almost overpowering her.

Gideon reached for the board and putting some oil on the rag, he began rubbing again. His movements soothed her and her thoughts slowed down.

"I don't want to do anything until after I go on my quest," she said after several quiet minutes. "Ever since I first planned to find that beautiful singer, problems have sprung up. You're not a problem, please don't think that. But there's a burning inside me to find her. Do you understand?"

"Yes, yes I do." He sighed and laid down his cloth. "I guess this means you'll want that wheelbarrow? I'll have it ready for you in a couple of days. But Susanna, promise me you'll think about marrying me, after you find the singer."

She looked at him shyly. "All right, I promise…to think about it. Don't forget to eat your cake."

Fidelity flew after Susanna as she left and gave another tiny shrug of her shoulders as she turned to look at Gustafus.

It was the morning of Susanna's quest and the sun had been up for an hour. Fidelity and Gustafus waited outside by the back door. They had listened to the breakfast chatter and now they saw Gideon come out and go inside the workshop. Soon he reappeared pushing the wheelbarrow towards the house. It was ready. Last night they had watched Susanna pack it for her journey. Now she came to the back door with her aunts behind her. She tucked her old boots in the corner of the wheelbarrow and covered them with an edge of the canvas top.

"I'm sure my good boots are enough," she said, "and I have two sets of laces, but I'll feel better with a second pair, just in case. Both of you are taking this well; I thought for sure you'd be upset and would try to talk me out of it."

The aunts exchanged a sheepish look.

"I told them there'd be no living with you if they didn't let you go," said Gideon.

"Well, this is it then," said Susanna, adjusting her shawl. "I'll be back before the fall, I imagine." Her eyes filled with tears as she looked at her aunts. The only time she'd been away from them was a night or two over at Amy's. She started to feel afraid and lonely. Thank goodness Gideon was going to walk with her as far as Aunt Violet's.

"Goodbye," said Aunt Prudence. "Say hello to Violet for me."

Aunt Maisy kissed her cheek. "Be back as soon as you can, dear."

Susanna lifted the handles of the wheelbarrow. Fidelity sat on the front edge balancing herself as Susanna tested the weight.

"I'm off."

The aunts watched her push it across the yard and then turn right onto the path to Violet's.

"This is a great wheelbarrow," said Susanna to Gideon. "Even though I've crammed it with stuff it still feels light and it balances easily. I have to confess I'm feeling nervous now that I'm really going to do this."

"You'll be fine," said Gideon.

"Have you ever been on a quest?"

"I'm on one right now."

She turned to look at him. "You mean you're on a quest because you've come away from your home?"

"No, I'm on a quest because I'm going home."

"You like to make mysterious statements, don't you?" she said, as she maneuvered the wheelbarrow around a stone on the path.

When they arrived at Aunt Violet's she came out the back door to greet them.

"Well, you certainly look like you'll have everything you need," she said.

"Yes, it's pretty full, but Gideon made it so it's easy to push. I guess this is it, I'm really off on my quest."

She looked at her aunt and then at Gideon.

"I'll say goodbye then."

"Goodbye Susanna," said Aunt Violet as she gave her a hug.

Susanna looked at Gideon. For the first time she saw uncertainty in his face.

"Goodbye, Gideon. Thanks for this splendid wheel barrow. It holds everything I need. I…I…well, goodbye."

Gideon tucked a fold of the tarp in tighter along the edge of the wheel barrow. "If you think you have everything you need then you'd better hurry on. The days are still short."

He looked into her eyes and she saw the sadness. He really

would miss her.

He took one of her hands, kissed it, covered it for a brief moment with his other hand and then let her go.

Susanna picked up the handles of the wheel barrow and started down the path beside the house. As she passed the front yard with the mirror between the cherry trees she stopped. She looked at the mirror and then looked at the gap between the hills.

I can't leave yet, she thought. I must find out what is at the top of that house I saw in my vision. It won't take me long. I'll just sit down on the courtyard steps for a few moments and try to find my music room. I'll stay away from those brambles, though; I don't have time to fool with them.

Susanna made herself comfortable on the top step and then closed her eyes. She knew she must find the room in her heart first before she could walk through the mirror. Heartfire breath in, heartfire breath out. The brambles appeared. Why do they come every time, she thought in frustration? I will not pay attention to them. I won't.

"Listen to me," said a small tendril sliding towards her along a vaporous pathway. "I have something so sad to tell you." And a sad feeling oozed from it and filled the pathway.

Susanna knew that feeling. It had lain hidden at the bottom of her fears.

Her days after her mother and father died came back to her in a stream of pictures. She saw their bodies, newly washed and clothed in their coffins. Why didn't they breathe, she thought and felt a suffocating feeling in her own body. Oh, I want them back, she cried as she hugged herself.

Another picture from her past came streaming into her mind. She was in her bedroom, lying on her bed, pretending to be asleep so her aunts would leave her alone. They had worried over her all day because she wouldn't eat. How could they expect her to eat when they'd just buried her mother and father? She heard their voices in the hall outside.

"She's asleep now, poor thing," said Aunt Maisie.

"We must be firm with her," said Aunt Prudence. "We'll make her eat properly and dress warmly all year round. She's just like her parents and we must make sure she never catches a chill. Perhaps she'll live to be a young woman if we take good care of her. She's all we have now."

"There, there," said Aunt Maisie, with a sniff.

"I know she's much too tall for that thin frame of hers. Oh, Maisie, why should a couple of old maids like you and I have strong constitutions?"

The voices faded away and Susanna lay on the bed staring into the dark. She was going to die like her parents. She would lie quiet and pale in a coffin and people would cry over her. And she would never have a long life.

Fear grew from a knot of sadness in her heart. It grew and covered the sadness. All that remained of the sadness was a tired, dull feeling that nothing mattered too much.

The pictures faded and the tendril of sadness sidled towards her. It started to creep up her leg, slowly as if not wanting to wake her from her memories. Behind the tendril came the twigs and then the main branch.

The droning increased.

"Why try," it said. "Just lie still, sleep, sleep, don't fight it. It will soon be over. Drop into this sad, sad feeling. Let it take you."

Susanna was about to fall into an uneasy sleep when she remembered the breeze of colors that had ruffled the grass around the coffins at the grave site. It had seemed so out of place at the time, like a happy, carefree breeze that didn't realize what had happened.

A door opened in her heart and a melody came through. It cleared her mind. She saw the tendrils slithering around her. She looked closer at them. Their surface was covered tightly with a smooth bark and on the bark moved the stream of pictures she had just remembered. She saw the last thought that had worried her drop into its place, bulge for a moment with sadness and then move slowly along.

Susanna realized what was happening. These were her thoughts! These were her brambles! She had made them and replayed them again and again throughout her life. Now they had come back to suffocate her—to cover her up and tuck her into a strange droning sleep. All her attention to them had given them life.

"No!" she shouted. "I will not fall asleep! Just because my aunts think I'll die young and just because I've believed it doesn't mean it's true. I will live! I will live forever! I'm sorry I made those awful thoughts but I'm bigger than those thoughts. I'm stronger and I will not lie down and die. I will take my attention off of you and you will shrivel up and disappear."

The brambles whimpered and cried out that she was killing them.

Susanna ignored them and looked into her heart. Then new pictures from her past streamed into her awareness. It was the day of her parent's burial. She watched as an invisible spectator.

Aunt Prudence was there, Aunt Maisie too, and Susanna, a younger Susanna clutching Aunt Maisie's hand. She watched the three of them walk back through the woods to the house. Then it was quiet by the grave site, so still that it felt like the whole earth was listening.

The breeze of colors wafted around the coffins. Then there was a sound as if a choir suddenly burst into song and a group of majestic people appeared in a circle of white light. They sang to her mother and father. Life was a song, they said, a song that went on and on, ever new, never ending. Nothing could stop it. The song could resurrect the life in each cell of their bodies. Listen to its beauty. Fill your bodies with its life.

Then her parents rose from each coffin, as if the wooden lids were not there. They were singing and their bodies were young, as young as she was now.

They sang a song she had never heard before.

Within our bodies, casting its spell,
Spring has sprung in every cell.
Resurrection is growing strong
Healing every seeming wrong,
Transmuting decay into light
And casting out the darkest night.
Each room of memories tired and old
Becomes a palace of light's stronghold.
The sound of bells ringing true
Echoes, echoes all the way through.
Nothing is left of sadness and gloom
And our new heart begins to bloom.
Now we're rising higher and higher
Completely filled with resurrection's fire.

Her parents joined the radiant beings and they all rose into the air and passed beyond her sight. Only the small breeze remained—a dancing breeze of gentle color that wafted towards her and twirled around her feet, spiraling upwards, touching her like a feather and pausing at her lips.

She breathed it in.

In the next instant she was inside the music room, sitting in her chair and marveling at the beauty of the flower before her with the diamond in its center. One of the facets caught her eye and she felt herself drawn through it as if she were no bigger than a thought.

She was on the pathway winding up to the pillared house.

When Susanna opened the front door she saw a difference—all the corners were swept clean. From above her came the music. It rippled down the stairway in a colored stream of liquid light, touching her feet and then twirling back up. She followed.

The halls and stairs became less distinct as the light grew brighter. Soon they disappeared altogether and in their place was a pillared walkway gradually circling upwards.

The walkway ended in a large circle of pillars. A ball of light like a sun hung high over the space spreading its radiance in a golden canopy. In the center of the circle was another tall mirror. The melody flowed in a gentle waterfall from the sun and spilled in a ring of light within the mirror.

She moved slowly towards it, wondering what she would see. It was her usual reflection superimposed on the ring of light—at first.

The melody became so sweet that she ached to drink it in, to let it fill her up. As she felt this she raised her arms. Then as she looked in the mirror the sun appeared to be shining through her and it was centered in her heart. The song radiated out from the sun clothing her in a rainbow garment. In that moment Susanna began to sing. She was this glorious voice singing powerfully like the rushing of many rainbow streams and then softly, like the still, small thoughts that had saved her from the brambles. Then there was silence. A silence that seemed pregnant with melodies unborn, unsung. Then Susanna knew who she was. There wasn't just a magic singer, there was a magic song. Her body was this glorious instrument that the song could flow through. She was the song and the instrument and the quiet blissful awareness of being all of it.

The mirror disappeared. Through the pillars she could see Gideon standing on the lawn outside the Mansfield home—the sunlit home she had seen in her first vision. He was singing—his eyes focused on something within himself. His voice made her think of blue skies and golden fields laden with happiness.

She began to sing with him. Her voice curled around his, touching, blending, yet always holding its own sound. He looked at her and she knew she loved him.

And then she was back, sitting on the top step of the courtyard. The mirror had disappeared from the lawn where it had sat between the cherry trees. It took a moment for Susanna to realize this and then to become aware of Aunt Violet beside her in the rocking chair.

She stood up and exclaimed, "Aunt Violet, I've seen the magic singer and the song! I am both, I am! I'd forgotten about. I used to know this when I was very little, but I forgot. I'm not this clumsy body, I'm not even all those worrisome thoughts and feelings.

"It's as if I've been asleep and now I'm waking up to whom I really am.

"Do you know what? This must be the true blending—not the other kind that Aunt Prudence always lectured me about, the becoming brown and ordinary, but blending this magic into all of me.

"Oh, Aunt Violet, I'm filling up with happiness." And with that Susanna sat down again and let the tears fall.

Her aunt sat beside her on the step and put an arm around her shoulders. "Well done, Susanna. I'm so proud of you. Everything depended on you discovering that you're much more than what you see in an ordinary mirror. I could give you some help with the shawl and with Fidelity helping but you had to do the rest by yourself. If you went on thinking that somewhere outside yourself there was a magic singer you had to find, my plan wouldn't have worked."

"Aunt Violet, I should have known you'd have a plan. It's probably out of this world."

"No, it's quite ordinary, if you'll excuse that word. I simply want you to get married and have children; to someone you love, of course." She removed her arm so she could look at Susanna.

"That's all?" said Susanna, searching for her handkerchief.

"That's the start. Susanna, I come from what people call the Secret Valley. So does Gideon and so do all the traveling singers."

"Then my mother came from the Secret Valley?"

"Yes and her marrying your father gave me this idea. You see, people outside the Secret Valley have forgotten who they are. They've let those droning brambles grow up around the Magic Song. That's all they hear most of the time. Without listening to the magic singing from their heart they start to dry up, like a garden that hasn't been watered. What people call ordinary is really dryness. The melody in our heart is the magic water that gives life to everything."

"Then that's what the plains need, the magic water," said Susanna, giving her eyes a final wipe with her handkerchief."

"Exactly. The land clothes itself with the music of our thoughts and feelings and reflects them back to us—dry, parched land reveals the inside desert. The idea behind the traveling singers was that they would compose songs to dispel the gloom, so people would begin to hear the melody of their inner singer. The problem has been that after the singers leave, people let themselves be lulled back to thinking they're ordinary. I even tried the same thing with my jellies and they too only work for a while. The drone of the usual thoughts and feelings is like a song too; but it's dull and heavy and makes people fall into a sleeplike state. But with you, my dear." Aunt Violet cupped Susanna's cheek gently with her hand. "You've seen and heard the magic song. You won't forget, because the door has opened and now it can never be shut."

"I'm getting the picture. You want someone who's going to stay in one place so the song can keep going out. That's why you started giving me singing lessons. Did you want me to get married, so I could teach my children?"

"Yes, that's it."

"My goodness," said Susanna, putting her hands to her cheeks, "I'm getting this incredible picture of being the start of a dynasty. You know, the many times great grandmother of a long line of singing children. It's like they're all lining up behind me and I'm leading them over the hills and through the valleys."

"That's the picture. But we must find you a husband,

they are necessary for dynasties. Let's see what we find in the kitchen."

Susanna blushed as she went down the steps and pushed her wheel barrow around to the back door. Then she walked into the kitchen. Gideon sat at the table. When she entered he searched her face intently. Then he let out his breath and smiled.

"Well?" he asked.

Susanna couldn't help grinning. "It seems I didn't have to travel as far as I figured for my quest and I didn't need a wheel barrow. Aunt Prudence and Aunt Maisy will be surprised to see me back so soon."

"Probably not," he said. "I told them Violet would talk you out of it, so they didn't need to kick up a fuss about your going off."

"You did! That's why they were so calm. Thanks for making it easy for me. Let's go home."

Aunt Violet walked them to the back door. "Isn't it wonderful where listening to jellies can lead?"

Susanna turned and gave her aunt a long hug. "I can't thank you enough."

"We'll see you both soon. Take your time walking back," she said, winking at Gideon.

Gideon lifted the wheel barrow. "I'll push it," he said.

When they reached Susanna's rock he turned from the path and placed the wheel barrow so that it leaned against a tree. She stood beside him as he straightened up. Gustafus gestured to Fidelity and they both withdrew into the trees to give the couple some privacy.

Gideon took both her hands in his and said, "Your Aunt Violet persuaded me to come with her on this trip. She said I'd find my true love. When I first arrived here I felt like I had a weight on my chest. It feels so much lighter in the Secret Valley than it does here. But when you came into the workshop that very first day, to ask me to build a wheelbarrow, and I saw your face, I felt as if I'd come home."

He touched her face gently with his hand. "It's as if your song is a sculptor who lovingly molded your face and when I look at it, I recognize something I've always been searching for—a part of myself. Well, what do you say?"

Susanna threw her arms around him and as she hugged him it felt like every part of her was tingling and when she closed her eyes she could see the tingles, all star bright, like sunlight on snow.

"I'll marry you!" she said.

She felt his sigh of relief and then he hugged her even tighter. "Susanna, Susanna," he murmured.

"Yippee!" said a little voice close to their ears. "At last!"

Fidelity hovered just behind Susanna. Gideon waved his hand at her and she put her hand to her lips. "Oh dear," she said. "I'll go back into the trees and talk to Gustafus." She whisked herself away.

"We'll live in your house," said Gideon.

"Of course"

"And we'll be married right away. I'm not waiting longer than a week."

"Two weeks," she said, nestling closer. "I want to make a really beautiful dress. It won't be ordinary. That's not the way I want to start my life with you."

"Two weeks and that's it then."

"Maybe I'll let Erna make some of her fancy bread. Aunt Maisy will be beside herself planning all the baking and Aunt Prudence will want to scour every inch of the house, even the attic and the closet under the stairs. Oh, I wish my mother and father were still alive. I really want them to see me get married and I want them to meet you."

Gideon let her go and took her hand. He led her to the rock and sat down beside her.

"Your parents will be there," he said. "But people won't be able to see them."

"What do you mean?"

"They've blended completely with their magic song and that makes them invisible to people living outside the Secret Valley."

"I still don't understand. And how would you know such a thing?"

"We're taught this when we're youngsters. The whole world is made up of music and there are many levels and each level is like an octave. Just as we can only hear a certain range of notes, so we can only see a portion of what's here. The whole reason for being here is to expand the song of your Singer into every part of you, into every part of your life and that raises your world into those higher ranges because that's the true home of our song. One day you find you have to rise even higher in order to keep expanding the song. That's when you find the space where the song lies quiet and undisturbed."

"Then that's it? I mean does anything interesting happen after that?"

Gideon pushed a thick curl over her ear with a tender motion. "Once you blend with your song the real fun begins. Then you can see octaves of music rippling out in all directions, like infinite trails of melody you can follow to discover more beautiful worlds. In the Secret Valley it's easier to follow where the music leads, not like here where people let heavy thoughts and feelings cover up the song in their hearts."

"Why would you want to marry me and live here then?"

"Because my song led me here. Susanna, I want to be with you and now that you know who you really are, we have so much more to share. We can really help change this land."

Susanna hugged him. "You're right. When I found my song, I found you, the real you. This is splendid. It feels like I'm married to you already and a ceremony hardly seems necessary. But, of course," she said, blushing as she released him, "we'll have a beautiful wedding. Not many people will come though. But I don't care, as long as you're there."

From the trees Gustafus turned to look at the couple. He rolled his eyes. "They'll be a while yet."

"Let's go tell all our friends," said Fidelity. "When we get back they'll be ready to go home, I should think."

Chapter Twelve

THE BEGINNING

On the morning of Susanna's wedding day her bedroom bustled with comings and goings. First, Aunt Maisy arrived with breakfast. Then Aunt Prudence whisked in to make sure she had eaten it.

"You'll need your strength," she said. "I wanted you to eat downstairs so I could keep an eye on you, but Maisy insisted on spoiling you." She straightened the already smooth bedspread and continued, "Why in the world you and Gideon want to spend the first days of your marriage camping out in the hills is beyond me. It's never been done before. Couples are supposed to start the first day of their marriage in the same ordinary way it's going to be for the rest of their lives. That's sensible, I think. Your father and mother stayed put on their wedding day. Mind you, after they'd been married for a while, they did take off for the hills some times and they'd be gone for several days. I think that cold mountain air weakened their lungs so when we had the year of bad colds they couldn't fight off the pneumonia."

Susanna looked at her aunt and recognized the worry in her voice. "Gideon and I have excellent lungs. No cold or anything else is going to carry us off. We intend to fill this house full of children. You'll be so busy you won't have time to worry."

"Surely you haven't discussed such things already!"

"No, but I know we'd both like that though."

Aunt Maisy walked in at that moment with her arms full of filmy material. "Your Aunt Violet dropped this off, dear. It's a veil, she said. It looks big enough to be a dress but, I swear, it's as light as a feather."

Aunt Prudence sniffed, "I'm not sure I approve of all this finery. Well, you'd better get that fancy dress on. People are going to be gathering soon."

Aunt Maisy helped her put the dress over her head and then watched as the white folds fell into place.

"Those tiny pink ribbons threaded through the lace bodice are very pretty, dear," said Aunt Maisy, "Don't you think so Prudence?"

Aunt Prudence pursed her lips.

Aunt Maisy rushed on, "It matches the lace around the cuffs and hems just perfectly. I'm sure everyone will admire it. After all, this is a special day and I'm sure no one will say anything critical." She frowned at Prudence.

"You help Susanna arrange that…that veil, Maisy. I'll see if everything is ready on the front lawn."

"It's all the excitement," said Aunt Maisy, after Prudence had left. "It makes her a little sharp. She'll be fine once everything is back to normal. Now, let's see if we can figure out how this veil is to be worn."

Susanna waited at the front door.

The door opened and Aunt Prudence stuck her head in. "The mayor is in position under the cherry tree. It's time to start."

Susanna began to walk slowly down the porch stairs. She was determined that she would not trip on this special day.

Fidelity flew before her, dressed in the same style of dress. As Susanna walked across the lawn, her veil streamed out behind her. To most of those watching it looked like layers of wispy net floated in the air, yet there was no breeze. Each layer of the veil was held by a row of fairies.

The moment she walked out the door she heard the music. Music was never heard at weddings. Tradition insisted that the ceremony was quick, without muss and fuss. But Susanna knew that few of those present would hear it because the fairies played it. They moved gracefully on either side of her, those with the instruments on one side and the singers on the other. She walked in time to the rhythm and listened to the words of the song.

We are gathered here today
To send these two on their way,
To a path that's full of song,
Words and tunes in a great throng.
Join we now these two sweet hearts,
With a love that will ne'er depart.
A new song begins this day,
Sweeping gloom and fear away.
Sing it soft and sing it low
Sing it now where ere they go.
For this world needs their love
To fall like rain from above,
Washing, cleaning, making new
So the finest dreams come true.

She soon stood beside Gideon. He took her hand and looked into her eyes. The mayor's voice droned the few ordinary words of the marriage ceremony. Soon he had finished and was pronouncing them husband and wife.

As Gideon lifted the veil from her face and gently draped it behind her, a new melody started in her heart. When he drew her into his arms and kissed her, the melody spread to every part of her.

In that instant, she felt she was outside of herself, watching. She saw the fairies lift the layers of her veil and shake them gently, as if they were delicate rugs. Colored ripples of the melody flowed out from each layer and rolled over the valley of Spring Gate. Everyone in the valley was touched by the music and she watched as each person softened, spoke more kindly, smiled for no obvious reason or just gave a relaxed sigh. They heard the melody not with their ears, but with their hearts.

Then she was back and Gideon had just given her another kiss, this time on her forehead. He turned her around in his arms so they faced their guests.

Aunt Violet stood up and started clapping. Then from the third row, Erna began clapping and everyone joined in. Soon the guests were lining up to congratulate them.

"What a lovely wedding," said Erna, giving Susanna a hug. "Weddings are usually such dull affairs, aren't they? Well, you'll be glad to have my new bread, won't you? You need something a little fancy on a day like today."

"I still say it would have been wiser to take the horse and wagon into the hills with you," said Aunt Prudence as they stood on the lawn in front of the courtyard at Aunt Violet's house. "You can't possibly have enough for two people in that wheelbarrow."

"Susanna has a fondness for it," said Gideon. "We'll be fine. We're off then. Look for us in a couple of weeks."

"Make sure you have a hot breakfast every morning," said Aunt Maisy.

"Keep warm," said Aunt Prudence.

Aunt Violet just smiled and waved.

Gustafus and Fidelity waved as well. "You would have thought we'd be allowed to go with them to the Secret Valley," said Fidelity, "but Violet said they needed to be by themselves."

By the time Gideon and Susanna reached the gap in the hills, Aunt Violet's house was out of sight. But Aunt Violet herself was waiting for them as they followed the trail through the opening.

"I had to travel with a special wind to make it here before you," she said. "Time for your gift. I've enlisted the help of the mountain wind fairies. No need for you to take up precious time traveling. Here we go."

She began to sing. A ribbon of color flowed from her

heart. Through the gap before them came the rushing of the wind, its sound like a many-voiced choir. Billows of color, ridden by fairies, met Violet's music and joined together. Her song changed and the billows flattened out into two streams of color that flowed under the wheelbarrow and supported it like the rails of a sleigh. The colors widened and flattened under Gideon's and Susanna's feet. The fairies lined up at the front of the wheel barrow holding the ribbons like reins and faced towards the Melody Mountains.

"See you in two weeks," said Aunt Violet. "Learn what you can, Susanna, and when you're back we'll carry on with our singing lessons. Hold on to the wheelbarrow handles. Off you go, now."

The fairies pulled on the ribbons, and the wheelbarrow with Gideon and Susanna balanced behind it, moved up and away, flying through the gap in the smoother hills, through the opening between the pine treed hills beyond, following Sweetwater Creek to the foot of the mountain and then up, up, up, past the rivulets and over Tunetall Peak to the sun-bright valley beyond.

THE END

www.ingramcontent.com/pod-product-compliance
Lightning Source LLC
LaVergne TN
LVHW051011080826
845145LV00009B/2562

* 9 7 8 1 7 3 4 3 8 3 8 0 5 *